*New York City just got a little hotter. . . .*

As the cab screeched into motion, Tom's lips found Elizabeth's. He kissed her passionately, with all the pent-up yearning he usually tried hard to hold back. It was unimaginably wonderful to know that for once he *wouldn't* be going back to his room alone and frustrated.

His hands ran down her arms, around her waist, and up the back of her sweater. Elizabeth shivered, and for a second Tom was afraid she was going to push him away. Then she sighed and seemed to melt against his chest.

*I feel like I've died and gone to heaven,* Tom reflected as they dissolved into another urgent, searching kiss. *And we're not even home yet!*

"Oh, Tom," Elizabeth gasped when they sat up and pulled apart for air. "I've never felt this way before!"

Tom gazed at Elizabeth, momentarily unable to speak. Her eyes were shining, her hair was tousled, and her face was flushed. Tom didn't think he had ever seen a more beautiful sight.

"Remember, this is just the beginning," he murmured, tracing the contours of her kiss-stung lips with his fingertip. "It's going to get even better."

Bantam Books in the Sweet Valley University series.
Ask your bookseller for the books you have missed.

And don't miss these Sweet Valley
University Thriller Editions:

*Visit the Official Sweet Valley Web Site on the Internet at:*

# http://www.sweetvalley.com

# SWEET VALLEY UNIVERSITY®

# *Elizabeth ♥ New York*

**Written by**
**Laurie John**

**Created by**
**FRANCINE PASCAL**

BANTAM BOOKS
NEW YORK · TORONTO · LONDON · SYDNEY · AUCKLAND

RL 8, age 14 and up

ELIZABETH ♥ NEW YORK

*A Bantam Book / June 1998*

*Sweet Valley High® and Sweet Valley University®*
*are registered trademarks of Francine Pascal.*
*Conceived by Francine Pascal.*
*Produced by Daniel Weiss Associates, Inc.*
*33 West 17th Street*
*New York, NY 10011.*

ISBN: 0-553-49223-3

*Published simultaneously in the United States and Canada*

*Bantam Books are published by Bantam Books, a division of Bantam*
*Doubleday Dell Publishing Group, Inc. Its trademark, consisting of the*
*words "Bantam Books" and the portrayal of a rooster, is Registered in*
*U.S. Patent and Trademark Office and in other countries. Marca*
*Registrada. Bantam Books, 1540 Broadway, New York, New York 10036.*

PRINTED IN THE UNITED STATES OF AMERICA

OPM     0 9 8 7 6 5 4 3 2 1

*To Isabella Rose Vaccaro*

# Chapter One

"My darling," Tom Watts whispered huskily as he gestured across the room with a sweep of his arm. "One day all this will be yours."

Elizabeth Wakefield giggled. "If this is all you've got to offer, I'll have to start looking for a new boyfriend."

"Ouch!" Tom exclaimed. "Too cold. You wound me!" He placed his hand over his heart dramatically and staggered backward as if her words had knocked the wind out of him. But his brown eyes twinkled mischievously, and a sly grin spread across his face.

Smiling, Elizabeth glanced around the modest, furnished one-room apartment that would be Tom's summer home. The place was small and a little run-down, but it was clean and cozy. Glass sliding doors spanned the entire back wall. A folded-out sofa bed and a dresser took up the right side of the room. In the middle of the room an ancient cabinet-style TV faced an overstuffed armchair. Other than a small kitchenette on the left and a few half-unpacked cardboard boxes strewn across the floor, the rest of the apartment was bare.

"I understand you're just looking out for the bottom line, Wakefield," Tom growled. He wrapped his muscular arms around Elizabeth's waist, making her skin tingle at his nearness. "Give me another chance—I have some other assets that'll sweeten the deal."

"Well, I might reconsider," Elizabeth allowed. "But only if I get an advance on some of those . . . assets." She planted an affectionate kiss on his cheek.

"Mmmm, nice," Tom moaned. "You can liquidate as many of *those* assets as you want." He leaned forward and brushed the nape of her neck with his lips.

When Elizabeth reached up to run her fingers through Tom's thick brown hair, he lowered his face to hers for another lingering kiss. She felt a delicious shudder run down her spine. For a moment she was transported away from the little apartment . . . away from everything but the feeling of Tom's lips on hers.

When they paused for breath, Elizabeth reluctantly shook herself back to reality. It scared her sometimes how easily she could get lost in Tom's kisses. Even though they'd been dating for ages, the electricity between them was as powerful as it had been the day they'd met.

Elizabeth and Tom were both students at Sweet

Valley University, and they'd gotten to know each other at WSVU, the campus TV station. Over time their shared passion for journalism and admiration for each other's work had evolved into head-over-heels love. They'd been planning to spend the summer together for months, and Elizabeth had been overjoyed when Tom found an apartment just a few blocks from her parents' house on Calico Drive.

"I'm just kidding about the apartment, of course," she said lightly. "This place isn't bad at all—especially for what you're paying."

"And I get to be near *you*." Tom tenderly traced the line of her jaw with his fingertip. "We're going to have the most awesome summer together, Liz. My internship is going to rock, and you and I are going to have a blast."

Elizabeth flinched slightly at the mention of Tom's internship. "I'm sure we will," she responded neutrally, giving Tom a tight smile.

Tom's *the one who's going to have the awesome summer, not me,* she lamented as she shrugged off Tom's embrace. *After all,* he's *the one with a great job and his own place while I'm stuck with my parents and a lame summer job. He's living an adult life—I might as well be back in high school!*

Tom had landed a plum summer internship at Action 5 News, a major network affiliate in L.A. Elizabeth had been planning to intern for *Inside Scoop*, a syndicated half-hour newsmagazine. But *Inside Scoop*'s ratings were down, and just as Elizabeth was finishing up her final exams, she'd

3

gotten a call from the producer saying their budget for summer internships no longer existed.

Of course, it was too late to apply for another internship, so Elizabeth had had to settle for a job at Pageturners, a local bookstore. Elizabeth had always loved to read, but being a store clerk wasn't exactly the summer job she'd had in mind. She'd been looking forward to enriching her experience in journalism, the career path she'd dreamed of taking all her life. And she hated being reminded of how Tom's summer job would look a *lot* better on a resume than hers.

"I am *so* psyched," Tom went on. "Can you even believe I start tomorrow? I totally lost track of time. I guess it's better this way—I haven't had time to get nervous."

Elizabeth turned to face her beaming boyfriend and wished she could push her jealousy aside. *You're not being fair,* she told herself. *You should be happy for Tom, not feeling sorry for yourself.*

"Why should I be nervous anyway?" Tom continued obliviously. "They're lucky to have someone with my experience on their team."

*Still, it would be nice if he could show a* little *understanding,* Elizabeth amended. *In fact, why doesn't he stop rubbing it in already?*

"Liz, is everything OK?" Tom asked. "You seem preoccupied."

Elizabeth shook her head. "I'm sorry, Tom. I'm just tired. I had a really long day."

"Oh, right—it was your first day at Pageturners, wasn't it?" Tom mentally kicked himself for rattling on about his job without asking Elizabeth about hers. "How'd it go?"

Elizabeth shrugged. "OK, I guess."

"That good, huh?" Tom studied her downcast face. He knew Elizabeth was disappointed about losing her internship, but now she looked downright depressed.

*Wait till she sees the surprise I have for her,* he thought, grinning with anticipation. *She'll cheer up for sure!*

Tom held out his arm. "Liz, close your eyes and take my hand," he instructed. "I want to show you something."

Elizabeth looked up in surprise.

"Go ahead," Tom urged her.

She accepted his hand and shut her eyes. "What's going on?"

"You'll see," Tom said mysteriously as he led her through the glass doors and into his backyard. His heart was doing flip-flops as they made their way down a path that led to the bank of a bubbling stream.

"OK, you can look now," he announced, watching Elizabeth closely as she opened her eyes. When her features lit up in delight, Tom felt his heart soar.

By the bank Tom had spread out an old lace tablecloth and set it like a formal dinner table. A large picnic basket in the center overflowed with a couple of baguettes, a bottle of sparkling water, several bunches of grapes, and wedges of Brie.

"Oh, Tom, it's so wonderful!" Elizabeth exclaimed. She threw her arms around him and planted a moist kiss on his lips. "This is *exactly* what I needed. Thank you."

Tom beamed. "I'm glad you like it," he said as he watched her sit down. In a silver blouse and a long black skirt that hugged her softly curving hips, Elizabeth looked so radiantly beautiful that his heart ached.

"It's so romantic," Elizabeth sighed. "You shouldn't have gone to all this trouble."

"Are you kidding?" Tom shook his head in disbelief as he knelt down across from her. "Liz, don't you know that you're everything to me? This is the *least* I can do to show you how much I love you."

Tom felt as if he hadn't known what love was before Elizabeth came into his life. For a long time after his family had tragically died in a car accident, Tom had been a loner, keeping all his emotions locked away. But Elizabeth made him feel whole again—not to mention incredibly lucky. Not a day went by that he didn't wonder what he had done to deserve a girlfriend who was not only gorgeous but sweet, intelligent, and caring as well.

"Why don't we dig in," Tom suggested gently, his heart pounding in anticipation of another surprise that was yet to come.

"Tom, what's this?" Elizabeth breathed, her eyes wide as she held up the small black velvet box.

"Open it."

"So I looked her right in the eye and I said, 'Excuse me, but are those Armani shoes? With a

Versace dress? Do you by any chance have a multiple-personality disorder?'"

"Lila, you did *not*." Isabella Ricci clapped a manicured hand to her mouth while Jessica Wakefield and Denise Waters shook their heads in disbelief. "So what did she say?"

"What *could* she say?" Lila Fowler set her cup of espresso on the table outside the chic ocean-side café, an expression of smug triumph on her face. "Obviously *we* got the table at Chez Soi."

"You're terrible, Li." Denise laughed, her wavy brown hair shimmering in the afternoon sunlight. "Sometimes I can't get over actually *knowing* someone like you."

Lila shrugged and patted her immaculate chignon. "Well, all's fair when it comes to love and dinner reservations. When my blood sugar is low, the claws come out. I'm only human."

Jessica took a sip from her mug of cappuccino and willed herself not to roll her eyes. *OK, so Lila may be my best friend and all,* she acknowledged silently, *but sometimes she* really *needs to get over herself.*

While Jessica had been looking forward to enjoying one last lunch with her sorority sisters before they left Sweet Valley for the summer, she was more than a little tired of hearing Lila monopolize the conversation. *I haven't even gotten to talk about* my *plans yet!* she thought with a pout.

"I'll have to get a few tips from you before I leave for London, Li," Isabella said. "I'm sure that attitude will come in handy when I'm interning for

7

Trevor Madson. Supposedly he has this sixth sense for fashion anxieties. I read in *Ingenue* that his last personal assistant had a nervous breakdown after he called her hairstyle passé."

*Helping a young British hunk design cutting edge fashions—that would have been my dream job a year ago,* Jessica reflected, setting down her mug and inspecting her black-and-white-striped minidress for coffee stains. *I would never have believed I'd find an even more glamorous way to spend the summer!*

"So, Jess." Denise speared a forkful of key lime pie. "Izzy's going to England, Lila's jetting to Paris, and I'm heading up to the San Francisco Culinary Institute. What's your secret destination?"

"Yeah, spill!" Isabella enthused.

Jessica straightened up proudly in her chair. "I'm going to the Sweet Valley Police Academy!"

"You're kidding," Lila said flatly.

"Are you serious?" Isabella chimed in. "They accepted you?"

Jessica's face fell slightly. "Um . . . *yeah.* I got the letter just the other day."

*OK, so I haven't exactly* received *the letter yet,* she clarified in her mind. *But I'm not lying—more like . . .* predicting! *The police academy is definitely going to want me. It's practically a done deal.*

"Jess, the police are around to protect and serve, not to pull over hot guys in fast cars," Lila reminded her. "Are you sure you're cut out for the force?"

"Of course I am!" Jessica retorted hotly. "I

8

happen to be very serious about this. And I'm totally qualified. This is going to be the most exciting summer of my life."

She couldn't believe her friends were being so unsupportive. She'd expected this kind of skepticism from her sister, Elizabeth; even though they looked identical, everyone who knew the Wakefield twins knew that Jessica was the fun, adventurous one while Elizabeth was a cautious, predictable bookworm. But Jessica's Theta sisters usually backed Jessica up when her own twin was a stick-in-the-mud.

*Why doesn't anyone think I can handle this?* Jessica wondered, glowering. She tried to console herself by smiling flirtatiously at a cute blond guy who was hanging around their table, but her heart sank when he scowled at her and pulled up the hood of his navy sweatshirt, hiding his face.

"Well, good luck, Jess." Denise shook her head. "I have to say, I'm glad I'll be baking soufflés instead of chasing bad guys."

Suddenly, before anyone had time to react, Sweatshirt Boy whisked Lila's purse off the back of her chair.

"My purse!" Lila screamed. "Stop, thief!"

In an instant Jessica was on her feet, propelled by sheer instinct. By the time she realized what she was doing, she was halfway down the block.

As she pounded down the pavement, every inch of her body pumping with adrenaline, Jessica saw the distance between herself and the thief closing rapidly. *Thank goodness I left my stilettos at home*

9

*today,* Jessica cheered mentally. *These platform sneakers put a righteous bounce in my sprint!*

Up ahead the guy turned a corner. Jessica kept running, ignoring the tightness in her chest. It wasn't as if Lila couldn't afford twenty replacement purses, but Jessica was determined to prove to herself, her friends, *and* the scumbag she was chasing that she was police academy material.

Jessica suddenly found herself in an alleyway lined with trash cans. The thief stopped dead in his tracks, obviously realizing he was cornered.

"Hold it right there, punk!" Jessica shouted. "You're totally busted!"

The guy snorted, reached into his jacket, and pulled out a switchblade. Jessica gulped as he waved the knife menacingly. *Think!* she told herself, racking her brain. *What would a cop do in this situation?*

Jessica jumped into a crouching position with her arm crooked over her head as if she were about to execute a karate move. It was a pose that she'd seen her favorite actress, India Jordan, use to roundhouse kick many a villain to death. But from there she had no idea what to do.

She glanced around desperately and spotted the trash cans. She lifted up two trash can lids and swung with all her might, bringing them crashing down on the creep's head. He let out an animal moan and toppled to his knees, dropping the knife.

"That'll teach you to mess with *me*," Jessica crowed, kicking the knife away and scooping up

Lila's purse. She heard a noise behind her and whirled around to see three police officers.

"Nice work, miss," one of them called as the other two hurried over to cuff the guy. "That was a very brave act. But you really shouldn't take the law into your own hands like that. Next time leave it to the professionals."

Jessica smiled. "Pretty soon I'll *be* one of the professionals!" she said giddily.

Elizabeth bit her lip as she opened the small black velvet box. Inside, nestled into neat folds of maroon satin, lay a slender gold bangle engraved with delicate, vinelike filigree work.

"Look on the inside," Tom urged softly.

Elizabeth lifted the bracelet from the box and held it up in the palm of her hand. On the underside were inscribed the words *Elizabeth, I love you forever. Tom.*

Tears welled up in Elizabeth's eyes. "Tom, it's . . . it's . . . ," she gasped, unable to get the words out. Staring at the inscription, she felt a stab of guilt for being jealous of Tom's internship.

"Do you like it?" Tom asked, sounding almost shy.

Elizabeth tore her eyes from the bangle and gazed up at Tom, her heart full. In the soft glow of twilight his tanned face looked angelic. "Tom, it's so beautiful," she breathed. "I don't know what to say."

Tom reached out and took the bangle from Elizabeth's hand. "I'm sorry I went on and on about my internship before," he said as he un-hooked the clasp. "I should have realized how it would make you feel."

Elizabeth held out her arm, and Tom fastened the bangle on her wrist. "I know your summer isn't going exactly the way you planned," he went on, "but I'm here for you, Liz. And I'm going to do whatever I can to make this the best summer of our lives."

A tear slid down Elizabeth's cheek. "Thank you—for everything," she whispered. "It means so much to know you understand."

Tom reached out and gently brushed away her tear with the side of his finger. Then he took both of Elizabeth's hands and laced his fingers through hers. "You're my world," he confessed, looking intently into her eyes. "Internship or no intern-ship, I vow to you that nothing's going to keep us from having a great summer together. I'm going to make you as happy as you make me—that's a promise."

"Oh, Tom, you already *have* made me happy," Elizabeth insisted. "And I know you're right—I'll get over losing the internship. As long as we're together we *will* have a wonderful summer."

For a moment she flashed on that day's hectic shift at the bookstore. At nine-thirty she'd already been counting the minutes until five. *Is looking for-ward to time with Tom really going to get me through the day?* Elizabeth wondered anxiously. *Through the whole summer?*

She pushed the thought firmly out of her mind as she leaned forward so her face was barely inches from Tom's. *If I really hate it, I can look for another job,* she reasoned. *In the meantime I should enjoy the here and now.*

As his lips met hers for a heart-stopping kiss, that suddenly didn't seem so hard.

# Chapter
# Two

"Coming through!" Tom panted as he burst out of the Action 5 News editing room, his head down like a linebacker's.

At the other end of the hallway, beyond a crowd of production assistants, the elevator doors were outlined like a bull's-eye. Feeling like Indiana Jones, Tom sprinted down the hall and barely managed to squeeze into the elevator before the doors slid shut.

*Less than a minute to noon,* he noted as the elevator sped up to the studio. *Why do they have to finish these edits so close to airtime?* If Tom didn't manage to get the footage of the day's lead story to the newsroom in thirty seconds, the twelve o'clock news anchor would be left with dead air—and Tom would get canned for sure.

As the elevator doors opened, Tom tore out into the corridor, deftly swerving to avoid a mail cart. The control room was all the way down the hall; by the time he reached the doors, the red On Air sign was flashing.

"Good afternoon," the anchor's voice blared from the monitors as Tom ran into the room. "In our top story, chaos broke out at city hall this morning. . . ."

"Tom, hurry!" the news editor hissed. Tom leaped across the room and pressed the tape into his outstretched palm.

"Action Five News has *this* special report," the anchor said gravely just as the editor slid the tape into a deck. An image of city hall appeared on the monitor, and Tom's shoulders slumped with relief.

John McGowan, the producer of Action 5 News, clapped Tom on the back. "Good work, Tom. You really came through for us. Next time I promise you'll get an assignment that tests your mind, not just your fifty-yard dash."

Tom grinned. "Thanks. I appreciate it."

"Why don't you head back to your desk and take a break before you start going through those archives?" Mr. McGowan suggested. "You've certainly earned a break."

Glowing with pride, Tom headed to his desk with a light step, momentarily forgetting how winded he was. *I'll give Elizabeth a call,* he thought. *She'll help me chill out—after all, there's no way her day could be as stressful as mine.*

"Pardon me, do you have this in paperback?"

Elizabeth looked up from the register to see a frail, elderly woman holding up an enormous hardbound book. On the book's cover a bronzed muscle man with long golden hair was unlacing the bodice of a buxom beauty in a red gown. *Savage Nights* was printed in gold foil letters across the top.

"I believe that's Jacqueline Kimberly's latest, ma'am," Elizabeth answered, stifling a smile. "I don't think it's out in paperback yet. You can find the rest of her books over by that back wall, though." She pointed toward the romance section.

"*Excuse* me, *I* was being *helped*," the balding man at the front of the line whined as he shoved his books toward Elizabeth.

"Yes, sir," Elizabeth mumbled, flushing as she turned back to the register.

*If this keeps up, I'm going to scream!* she thought in agitation. Pageturners had been mobbed all morning, and it seemed as if the more crowded the bookstore got, the crabbier every single customer became.

She picked up the paperback on top of the pile and swept it across the scanner. It didn't register. She swiped it again, and it made a loud error noise.

"I'm going on my break," announced the cashier on Elizabeth's left, a sixteen-year-old girl with a ring in her eyebrow. "This register's closed. Use her line."

A half-dozen indignant, muttering people crowded into the already too long line at Elizabeth's register.

"I was ahead of you!" somebody shouted.

*Oh no!* Elizabeth thought, panicking. *How am I*

*going to ring everyone up before they start a riot?*

The scanner made another angry buzzing noise. Giving up, Elizabeth picked up the next book with shaking hands.

"Elizabeth!" a sharp voice bleated. Mr. Mercado, the daytime manager, was standing at her elbow. His lips were pursed as if he'd been drinking lemon juice.

"Yes, sir?" Elizabeth replied timidly.

"You have a phone call." Mr. Mercado's gaze passed over the rowdy mob in front of Elizabeth's register. "I'll take over your station," he offered sourly.

Elizabeth sprinted to the phone at the other end of the counter. "Hello?"

"Hi, honey," Tom's cheerful voice sang over the line. "How's your day going?"

Elizabeth felt her tension level mount at the calm, contented note in Tom's voice. *"Busy,"* she replied curtly. "I can't talk. I have a million people waiting."

"Oh, OK, I'll let you go," Tom said lightly. "I just wanted to see if you felt like going out tonight—"

"Fine, great. Talk to you later, all right?"

"Pick you up at six?"

"OK. Good-bye." Elizabeth hung up abruptly and dashed back to the register.

Mr. Mercado gave Elizabeth a disapproving look as he let her take over the register. "Miss Wakefield, you haven't worked here very long," he said loudly. "I hope you'll learn to confine your personal life to your free time."

Elizabeth's cheeks burned. For once the people in line were silent. She could feel them staring at her. "Of course, sir," she said, forcing a smile. "I'm sorry."

*He has some nerve, chewing me out in front of customers,* she fumed as Mr. Mercado hurried to answer the phone again. She swiped a book of one hundred and one golfing tips across the scanner angrily.

"Elizabeth!" Mr. Mercado hollered.

Elizabeth spun around, momentarily worried that she had somehow been thinking out loud.

"You have *another* phone call," Mr. Mercado hissed.

Elizabeth gulped and ran for the phone, unable to meet her manager's eye. *I can't believe Tom is doing this to me,* she thought furiously. *I told him how busy I was!*

She snatched up the receiver. "Tom, *what?*" she snapped.

There was a pause on the other end of the line. "Um . . . is this Elizabeth Wakefield?"

Elizabeth had the sinking realization that she'd just made a big mistake. The caller's voice was vaguely familiar, but she couldn't quite place it. "Yes, this is she," she answered uneasily.

"Congratulations, Elizabeth—you've won the Miller Huttleby Fellowship!"

Jessica threw off the covers and swung her legs over the side of her bed in one motion. Shoving her feet into her pink slippers, she pulled on her fuzzy blue bathrobe and began humming the theme song to *Mission: Impossible*. She paused in front of her door and glanced around stealthily before opening the door and jumping out. She landed in the middle of the hallway with her arms outstretched, her fingers steepled as if she were pointing a gun.

"Freeze, sucker!" Jessica shouted in her best tough-as-nails policewoman voice. She fired off a few imaginary rounds, bounded down the stairs, and threw open the front door. Golden afternoon sunlight streamed into the house.

As she approached the Wakefield mailbox she could barely contain her excitement. It had been three weeks since she had sent in her application to the police academy, and all the forms had said she'd receive a response in two to four weeks. "Today's the day," she murmured as she lifted the lid of the mailbox. "I just have this feeling."

OK, so she'd had a "feeling" *every* day for the past week. For the first few days after the two-week mark passed, Jessica had paced around anxiously all morning until the mail arrived. Since then, in the interest of stress management, she'd taken to strategically sleeping until the afternoon.

Jessica extracted the large bundle of mail from the box. Shivering with excitement, she began rifling through the envelopes as she walked back to the house. There was a gardening catalog for Mom, a law review for Dad, a thick manila envelope for Elizabeth, a couple of bills, an express package, some supermarket circulars, and one crisp white envelope with the police department's seal in the corner.

"*Yes!*" Jessica crowed, jumping onto her tiptoes.

"I'm in!" She dumped the rest of the mail into a basket by the door. As she sprinted up to her room, the precious letter clutched to her chest, she could already see herself in her tailored navy blue uniform, looking sexy and powerful. She made a mental note to buy some understated silver stud earrings to accent her badge.

Her heart thumping wildly, Jessica sat down on her bed, tore open the letter, and scanned it eagerly.

> Dear Ms. Wakefield,
>     We regret to inform you that we are unable to admit you to the summer session of our officers' training program. Enrollment for the semester was filled early. We will keep your application on file and encourage you to reapply for the fall. . . .

Jessica's vision blurred with angry tears. "Reapply?" she sobbed, throwing the letter aside. "But I want to be a police officer *now!*" She flopped back onto her bed and stared blankly at the ceiling through her tears. "It's so unfair," she moaned.

For once Jessica had set out to do something really meaningful, and where had it gotten her? Stuck in Sweet Valley—where she'd spent practically every summer of her life—doing absolutely *nothing*.

*Maybe a boring job shelving dull, dusty books is OK for a pathological nerd like Elizabeth,* Jessica thought miserably. *But if I don't do something exciting with my summer, I'll go stark raving wacko!*

\*     \*     \*

"Wha—who is this?" Elizabeth stammered. "I— I didn't apply for any fellowship!"

"Elizabeth, this is Professor Timms. You were in my modern dramatic theory seminar this past semester?"

"Oh, of course," Elizabeth said. "Sorry, I couldn't place your voice. But . . . what is this about a fellowship?"

"The Miller Huttleby Foundation evaluates one-act plays by collegiate playwrights nationwide," Professor Timms explained. "Every year three remarkable students are flown to New York and given a budget to produce and direct their plays. Congratulations, Elizabeth—you've been selected as one of them."

"But Professor Timms, I'm *not* a playwright; I'm a journalist," Elizabeth protested. "Are you sure you haven't called the wrong student?"

The professor chuckled. "No, no, Elizabeth. Do you recall your final project for our class?"

"Oh—of course," Elizabeth answered, glad the professor couldn't see her blush. The assignment had been to write a one-act, one-set, two-character play. Elizabeth had completely blanked on what to write about until she and Tom had had a major argument. That night she'd stayed up until dawn writing *Two Sides to Every Story,* a play about the troubled relationship between two competing journalists. Professor Timms had raved about the "passion" and "raw emotion" in her dialogue, making Elizabeth feel slightly sheepish.

"Forgive me if I've overstepped my boundaries,

Elizabeth, but I felt that your play deserved attention," Professor Timms went on. "I went ahead and submitted *Two Sides to Every Story* to the foundation. I didn't tell you—the process is fiercely competitive, and I didn't want to get your hopes up for nothing. But lo and behold, you're headed for New York! The program starts in a week."

"New York? A week?" Elizabeth echoed. "But that's so soon! I can't. . . . How will I . . . where would I . . ."

*An incredible experience . . .*

*Produce my own play . . .*

*Once-in-a-lifetime opportunity . . .*

*But I can't just move to New York!* she concluded. After all, she was the responsible, stable twin. Jessica was the one prone to impulsively dropping everything to pursue some new scheme.

"If you're worried about the cost, the fellowship includes first-class airfare, a modest daily stipend, and of course a reasonable budget for production costs and actors' fees," Professor Timms explained. "I know it's a lot to take in at once. But this is a very prestigious honor."

*An honor that would look* great *on my resume,* Elizabeth realized. *I'd be doing something really worthwhile with my summer. I wouldn't have to work at this lousy bookstore. . . .*

*Bookstore!* Elizabeth suddenly became aware of just how long she'd been on the phone. "Professor Timms, I really have to get back to work. But I'll think about it—I just need a little time."

"All right, Elizabeth. You should be getting a

packet in the mail with further details. Think it over, talk to your parents, and call the foundation when you reach a decision."

"I will," Elizabeth promised. "It's a very exciting offer, Professor Timms. But I have to make sure it's what's right for me."

"He *thinks* he is all that and a bag of chips," a big-haired woman in a halter top declared as she snapped her fingers decisively, "but he is a *dog,* and I'm kicking him to the curb!" Wild applause erupted around her.

"You *go,* girlfriend," Jessica urged through a mouthful of cereal. She was on her third bowl of Sugar Frosties, and *Tease-n-Tell,* the sleaziest afternoon talk show on the air, was just getting warmed up.

Since reading the letter from the police academy, Jessica had lost the will to do anything but consume empty calories and destroy brain cells. After watching segments on topics like "My Sister Stole My Husband" and "Psychic Strippers Make Celebrity Predictions," she had already forgotten most of what she learned in her last semester of college.

"Well, we have a surprise for you," announced Jenny Tracey, the host of *Tease-n-Tell.* "When we come back, we'll meet your man's *other* woman!"

As a commercial for floor wax came on, the phone rang. Jessica muted the TV and reached for the cordless. "Hello?"

"Jess, it's me."

"Hey, Liz, how——"

"Listen, I need to ask you a favor."

"Gee, my day's *super*, thanks for asking," Jessica retorted sarcastically. "Except for the part where I got rejected from the police academy."

"You did? Oh, Jess, I'm so sorry!" Elizabeth apologized. "I didn't mean to be rude. It's just that I'm at the bookstore, and I'm going to get in trouble if I stay on the phone. Can you just do this one thing for me?"

"Fine." Jessica sighed. "What do you want?"

"Could you check the mail and see if there's anything from the Miller Huttleby Foundation?"

"OK, hang on." Jessica padded to the front door. Holding the cordless phone in the crook of her neck, she flipped through the basket of mail. She paused at the large manila envelope addressed to Elizabeth. "Yeah, this is it. Do you want me to open it?"

"No . . . I'll open it when I get home. I just wanted to make sure it was really true."

"Make sure *what's* really true, Liz?" Jessica demanded, lifting up the package in an attempt to see through the envelope. Then her eye lit on something resting in the basket.

"I'll explain when I get home, Jess," Elizabeth answered impatiently. "I have to go, OK?"

"Uh-huh. Later," Jessica replied, distracted. Ordinarily she'd have demanded to know what her sister was being so mysterious about. But she'd just noticed something very interesting: The express package was addressed to *Ms. Jessica Wakefield*.

\*　　　\*　　　\*

25

*Even the coffee here is perfect,* Tom thought as he set his steaming mug of hazelnut French roast on the intern desk and looked over the day's sports pages. *This is definitely the best job I've ever had.* Sitting alone in a spacious office with his tie loosened, Tom felt like a prominent news anchor. Sure, the morning had been hectic, but he'd gotten great feedback—everyone treated him like a professional.

"Hey there, Tom." Mr. McGowan popped his head through the doorway of Tom's office. "How's everything going?"

"Great!" Tom answered sincerely. "I've never learned so much in one day."

Mr. McGowan smiled. "I'm glad to hear that, Tom. It's gratifying to work with an intern who brings so much enthusiasm to the job. I just came in to tell you we've pretty much wrapped up the evening's segments. So feel free to take off whenever you'd like."

"Are you sure?" Tom asked. "I could stay if you need me."

Mr. McGowan waved his hand. "No, no, you've learned enough for one day. Go home, relax, let it sink in. I'll see you bright and early tomorrow, kid."

*I can't believe he just gave me the rest of the day off,* Tom marveled as he packed up his briefcase. *This really* is *my dream job. I can't wait to tell Liz all about it!*

*Should I go to New York?* Elizabeth wondered, her mind racing a mile a minute as she swiped books across the scanner. Practical as she was,

Elizabeth couldn't help thinking the opportunity was almost *too* good to be true. Could she really just pick up and leave with a week's notice? Could she really make it on her own in New York?

"I need that cookbook for my Fourth of July barbecue," the woman at the front of the line snapped. "I'd appreciate it if you could ring it up before, say, *Christmas*."

Elizabeth looked down at the book in her hand and realized she'd been holding it absently in midair. She rang up the book and put it into a plastic bag, apologizing profusely.

*Supposedly New Yorkers think Californians are too "nice,"* Elizabeth thought. *If that's true, then I probably can't handle New York!*

But even though the prospect of being alone in New York City seemed frightening, Professor Timms had as much as told her she'd be an idiot to pass up the fellowship. *It's not like I would be giving up a good job here,* Elizabeth reasoned. *Maybe I should just take a chance for once in my life. Why should Jessica be the only one who gets to be spontaneous?*

"Elizabeth!" Mr. Mercado bellowed. "Are you moving in slow motion?"

Elizabeth cringed. Once again she'd been so wrapped up in her thoughts that she'd lost track of what she was doing. She hadn't even noticed Mr. Mercado approaching.

"I expect a one hundred percent effort from every member of my team," Mr. Mercado lectured loudly. "I am *extremely* disappointed with what I have seen here today, Elizabeth. I ought to fire you on the spot. Is that what you want?"

The whole bookstore had gone quiet. Aware that all eyes were on her, Elizabeth felt her face grow hot. *If this is how Mr. Mercado treats me on my second day,* she thought indignantly, *this whole summer is going to be a nightmare!*

Elizabeth's eyes widened as she continued on that train of thought. She could stay here and be miserable, or she could . . . But *could* she?

Elizabeth glanced around the bookstore. She looked back at Mr. Mercado's enraged face.

The final decision took about five seconds.

"You can't fire me," Elizabeth announced. "I *quit*. I'm going to New York!"

_____

" 'The Florida Specialized Security Academy is one of the nation's foremost training facilities for private security professionals,' " Jessica read aloud. " 'Many of our graduates work as highly paid bodyguards to the stars; others join elite, top-secret agencies.'

"Stars!" Jessica squealed, kicking her feet in the air. "Elite, top-secret agencies!" She held the brochure up over her head and stared at the picture of Vince Klee, possibly *the* hottest actor on Earth, flanked by a gorgeous guy in a black leather jacket and a red-haired woman in a slinky black cat suit.

*That could be* me *in that cat suit,* Jessica thought with delight. *That could be* me *guarding Vince Klee's hot body! Action, excitement, glamour—this place looks even* better *than the police academy!*

She turned the brochure over and saw a picture of a hunky, muscular man in a black karate *gi* executing a kick in midair. Beside him was a woman in a black tank top, carrying a gun that looked like something Jessica had seen in a futuristic action movie. The brochure explained that FSSA provided training in martial arts, weapons technology, and surveillance.

"Cooool," Jessica breathed.

She sat up on her bed and sifted through the massive pile of materials FSSA had sent. There were several other brochures, all featuring pictures of attractive people who looked as if they had stepped out of a James Bond movie. Many of the pictures showed men and women dressed in black, silhouetted against palm trees at sunset.

Jessica could already imagine hitting the Miami nightclubs after a day of kung fu classes. She pictured herself in a sleek black velvet cat suit and high-heeled leather boots, deftly wrestling a gun from some crazed, Vince Klee–obsessed fan.

*"Jessica, you saved my life,"* Vince would whisper, his eyes filled with gratitude and adoration. *"How can I ever repay you?"*

Jessica smiled. "Ohhh, where would I *begin?*" she purred. "Well, it certainly *wouldn't* involve eating doughnuts and writing out parking tickets, that's for sure."

Beneath the brochures Jessica found a letter from the director of FSSA.

Dear Ms. Wakefield,

The Florida Specialized Security Academy is a training ground for the select few who have what it takes to work in the field of professional security. Jobs in this field have on average higher salaries and greater opportunity for advancement than jobs on the police force.

"It *is* better than the police academy!" Jessica exclaimed. "Vince Klee *and* more money? Where do I sign up?"

An investment in FSSA is an investment in your future. Our reasonable tuition of ten thousand dollars will provide you with the skills you need to work as a professional bodyguard or security officer.

*"Ten thousand dollars?"* Jessica screeched, the rosy Miami sunset in her mind beginning to fade. "But there's no way I can come up with that money!" Anxiously she skimmed the rest of the letter.

Because we at FSSA have identified you as an extremely promising candidate, we are pleased to provide a small measure of financial assistance in the hopes that it will make it easier for you to accept our offer.

"Financial assistance?" Jessica looked up from the letter, puzzled. She scanned the papers and brochures strewn across her bed. Then her eyes lit on a sealed envelope. When she grabbed it and tore it open, her jaw dropped.

"Is this, like, a scholarship?" she asked in amazement as she stared at the certified check for thirty-five hundred dollars made out to *Ms. Jessica Wakefield*.

"Liz, I'm so glad you're home!"

Elizabeth looked up from her Miller Huttleby Foundation brochure. "Don't you ever knock?" she asked her bathrobe-clad sister, who stood in the doorway to her room with a bundle of papers clutched gleefully to her chest.

"I got a thirty-five-hundred-dollar scholarship to the Florida Specialized Security Academy!" Jessica went on breathlessly. "I don't need the police academy—I'm going to Miami to be a bodyguard to the stars!"

"Thirty-five hundred dollars?" Elizabeth repeated. "A bodyguard? Jess, are you really sure—"

"Check this out, Liz." Jessica hurried over to Elizabeth's bed and held out a handful of papers. "You're going to *die* when you see these brochures!"

Suddenly Jessica looked down at Elizabeth's paper-strewn bedspread. "Liz, is this what you got today?" she asked. "What's going on?"

Elizabeth smiled and filled Jessica in on how she'd found out about winning the fellowship and impulsively quit her job. "I just decided then and there to go for it," she concluded, shaking her head. "So now I guess I'm stuck with my decision, huh?"

"Stuck? Liz, you've got it made!" Jessica sat down with a thud at the foot of the bed. "Your own play off-Broadway . . . it's the chance of a lifetime! I'm so proud of you for blowing off that loser manager and that boring bookstore. For once in your life you're handling things the way *I* would handle them."

"Why does that *not* reassure me?" Elizabeth asked dryly.

Jessica dumped her bundle of papers onto the bedspread and swatted her sister with a pillow. "You watch it," she warned. "You're messing with a soon-to-be trained assassin."

"Jessica, the thought of *you* being trained to kill is beyond scary," Elizabeth said with a giggle. "Now run this by me again. *Who* gave you a scholarship?"

"The Florida Specialized Security Academy," Jessica explained. "They train people to be body-guards for celebrities and, like, secret agents. And they want *me* so badly that they sent a check for three and a half Gs." She hugged her knees to her chest. "Isn't it amazing, Liz? Both of us getting these incredible offers in the same day?"

"Well, it does sound exciting," Elizabeth admitted. "But maybe it's *too* good to be true. Are you sure they're legit?"

Jessica waved aside the suggestion. "Liz, you're always looking for a catch. Let's just take a chance! What have we got to lose? We've got nothing better to do this summer."

"I guess you're right," Elizabeth agreed. "There's no way I'm crawling back to that book-store. I might as well bite the bullet and go to New York."

*New York.* A grin crept slowly across Elizabeth's

face. Jessica's energy was infectious; Elizabeth was actually starting to feel *excited* about doing something impulsive. "Yeah! I'm going to New York! And I have no clue what I'm going to do once I get there!"

"That's the spirit!" Jessica exclaimed, jumping up from the bed. "You've convinced me. Now I'm going to bite my own personal bullet and go deposit this check before the bank closes." She removed a carefully folded square of paper from the pocket of her bathrobe. "Liz, can I borrow your black turtleneck today? I feel the need to look stealthy."

Elizabeth rolled her eyes. "Fine, Jess. Just try not to get any pesky bullet holes in it. You know they're impossible to get out."

"I'm sure I'll learn how at FSSA," Jessica said breezily as she rummaged expertly through Elizabeth's bureau. "Thanks, Liz. I'll be right back!"

*Sometimes I don't know what I'd do without Jessica,* Elizabeth thought affectionately as her sister skipped back to her bedroom. *I'm glad she helped me decide to go to New York. It really* is *the chance of a lifetime!*

Feeling happy and relieved, Elizabeth reached for the phone on her nightstand to call Tom. She picked up the receiver and started to punch in his number, freezing as the full impact of her decision hit her like a brick to the stomach.

*Tom and I promised to be together this summer,* she reminded herself as she slowly hung up the phone. *Tom vowed that nothing would keep us apart.*

34

*How can I turn my back on him to go to New York?*
She'd been right after all—there *was* a catch.

"Do you want another bite of my caramel apple?" Tom asked.

"Thanks, but the funnel cake was pretty filling." Elizabeth smiled as they walked hand in hand between the cotton candy stands and ringtoss booths of the neighborhood street fair. Her hair was loose around her face, and in the rosy light of the setting sun it looked to Tom like spun gold.

As usual Elizabeth looked understatedly sexy, and the effect drove Tom wild. Over her straight knee-length gray skirt she was wearing a man's white collared shirt with the top two buttons undone, and he had to fight the impulse to stare shamelessly at the exposed glimpse of tanned collarbone. *I have the most beautiful girlfriend on earth,* he thought, gazing at Elizabeth with admiration.

"I'm really glad we came here." Elizabeth squeezed his hand. "I'm having a lot of fun."

The scent of Italian sausage wafted through the air. Jaunty carousel music played in the distance. Every few seconds the roller coaster swooped past with a rumble and high-pitched shrieks.

Tom took another bite of his caramel apple and gazed out at the sunset, savoring the buttery-sweet taste in his mouth and the scents and sounds around him. "This is the perfect end to a perfect day," he said contentedly. "I wish you could have seen me at the station, Liz. I've never been this excited about a job."

"Good for you."

Tom beamed. "I feel like the luckiest guy in the world. I have a great job, a great apartment, and best of all, I have the *greatest* girlfriend."

Elizabeth was silent. Was she still upset about losing her internship? "The only thing that could possibly make things more perfect," he declared, "would be if my wonderful girlfriend had a job that was as incredible an opportunity for her as mine is for me."

Elizabeth cocked her head and looked at him curiously. A slow smile spread across her face. "Funny you should say that," she began, launching into a story about something that had happened to her at the bookstore. Something about her boss chewing her out for talking on the phone . . .

*Poor Liz,* Tom thought sympathetically. *She doesn't deserve to be treated like that. I'm so lucky to be working with professionals.* As he gazed at the fairy-tale glow of the fair lights against the hazy California dusk, Tom couldn't remember the last time he'd felt so contented, so much at peace.

"Tom, did you hear what I just said?" Elizabeth asked. Her impatient, expectant look snapped Tom out of his faraway state.

"Sorry," he apologized with a sheepish grin. "I drifted off for a sec. What were you saying?" He took a large bite of his caramel apple.

"I won a fellowship," Elizabeth began slowly, "from the Miller Huttleby Foundation. They're sending me to New York City for the summer."

Tom choked on his apple.

\*       \*       \*

"Tom, are you OK?" Elizabeth pounded hard on his back with her palm. "Raise your hand if you need the Heimlich maneuver!"

"I'm fine," Tom wheezed, shaking his head. "I just need to sit down."

Elizabeth steered him toward a bench, where he collapsed beside her with several short, barking coughs.

"New York, huh?" he repeated.

Elizabeth nodded. "New York. For the summer."

Tom sighed, slumped his shoulders, and stared wordlessly at the ground.

Gazing out into the distance, Elizabeth tried to think of something to say. She watched the Ferris wheel until it was nothing but a blur of tiny white twinkling lights against the red-orange blaze of the sunset.

"I'm sorry, Tom—I know this comes as a surprise," Elizabeth said, covering his hand with hers. "But it's a once-in-a-lifetime chance. Think about it—I'd get to produce and direct my own play off-Broadway."

Tom sat up slightly and straightened his shoulders as if he was trying to regain his composure. "It sounds exciting enough," he said slowly. "But you're a journalist, Liz—not a producer, not a director, not a playwright. In the long run what good would dabbling in the theater for a summer do you?"

Elizabeth flushed as she grew slightly incensed. The way Tom said *dabbling*—it sounded so patronizing, as if she were only capable of playing around instead of doing valid, creative work.

"Well, it's not like working in the bookstore is exactly improving my career prospects," Elizabeth pointed out evenly, not wanting to let Tom's skeptical remark get to her. "And so what if I want to try something different? It's not every day that an expenses-paid trip to New York falls into my lap."

"Liz, you're not looking at the whole picture," Tom said, his voice taking on the infuriatingly condescending tone he occasionally used at WSVU. "I'm surprised at how naive you're being about this. There's more at stake here than your resume! Have you thought about where you're going to live? How you're going to find your way around? New York isn't like California, Liz—it's a tough place."

"Tom, I am *not* a little girl!" Elizabeth cried indignantly. "I *think* I'm capable of taking care of myself, even in a new city. And I'm certainly not going to miss out on an incredible summer because it'll involve doing something I've never done before."

"Oh, come on—"

"No, *you* come on!" Elizabeth countered. "Listen to yourself, Tom. Just a few minutes ago you were wishing I had a great job like yours—and now that I *do*, you're acting like I can't handle the challenge!"

The comeback seemed to shake Tom's foundations for a second. Then he took a deep breath. "Liz, I'm just saying that you should think about whether you want to fly across the country to put on a *play*," he said laboriously, sounding more patronizing than ever. "It's scary to pick up and leave your family and friends. You have to be sure this is *really* what you want."

"I *am* sure," Elizabeth declared, tossing her golden hair defiantly over her shoulder. "Tom, I love you, and the thought of us being apart all summer breaks my heart. But this is a chance I can't pass up. Could you please *try* to understand at least?"

Tom's brown eyes searched her face for a long moment. "It sounds like you've already made up your mind," he said softly.

Elizabeth nodded slowly. "Yeah, I think I have."

Tom glanced away for a second. "Promise me one thing, Liz," he said resignedly. "Just sleep on it until tomorrow, OK? If you still want to go, I'll understand." His voice broke slightly. "But considering that we both swore nothing would keep us apart this summer, I think you owe it to me— to *us*—to really think this through."

Elizabeth's eyes filled with tears. "Of course, Tom," she whispered. "Of course I promise."

"Don't worry—we'll get through this somehow," Tom whispered, leaning forward to kiss her tenderly on her forehead. When he drew back, Elizabeth smiled at him through her tears.

Deep down she knew she wouldn't change her mind. Now that Tom had questioned her ability to take care of herself in New York City, Elizabeth was determined to prove to him—and to herself—that she *could* handle it.

*Maybe the theater* isn't *my thing,* Elizabeth allowed silently. *But I can't give up this opportunity— not for Tom, not for anyone.*

# Chapter Four

"Of all the impetuous, illogical, irrational, immature, *insane* things you've ever done," Mr. Wakefield thundered, his knuckles rapping on the kitchen table for emphasis, "this has to be the absolute *worst*, Jessica."

Jessica threw her hands up in exasperation. She'd been arguing with her parents about the FSSA for the better part of an hour, and as far as she could tell, they were only interested in reminding her of every mistake she'd ever made in her life.

"Dad, that is *so* unfair," Jessica protested. "This isn't like that time—well, OK, *all* those times I borrowed your credit card without asking. This is something that I want to do to, you know, *improve* myself. Don't you guys get that?"

Ned Wakefield kneaded the bridge of his nose between his thumb and forefinger. With his hardly graying dark brown hair and brown eyes, he strongly resembled the twins' older brother, Steven, but right now he looked much older than usual. "Of course I understand, Jessica. In fact, I'm proud you're setting goals for yourself. But you should *never* have deposited thirty-five hundred dollars of someone else's money without consulting us!"

"Now you're committed to a program you know next to nothing about," Mrs. Wakefield added, "and you've entered into a financial agreement with no idea of the terms. For all you know, they could already be charging you interest on that thirty-five hundred. Did that even *occur* to you, Jessica?"

Glancing back and forth between her parents, Jessica gulped. The vein in her father's temple looked as if it were going to burst. Alice Wakefield, blond and blue-eyed like her daughters, had pinched her pretty face into a disapproving grimace. Jessica had the distinct sense that she was on trial . . . and about to be convicted.

*Mom has a point,* Jessica grudgingly admitted to herself. *Being in massive debt is scary. But it's one of those* faraway *scary things, like gray hair, or nuclear war, or final exams.*

Banishing all worries from her mind, she lifted her chin and tossed her hair over her shoulder. She knew that parents were able to smell fear, so she vowed to act as confident as possible. "I know *exactly* what I'm doing," she declared. "I deposited the money because I *wanted* to commit. I'm making a . . . a . . . an investment in my future!"

42

Mr. Wakefield sighed wearily. "What do you think *college* is, Jessica? We're already making an investment in your future—a rather *expensive* investment, in fact." He leaned back and steepled his fingers thoughtfully in a gesture Jessica called The Lawyer Pose. "Jess, I know you feel like you want this for the right reasons. But you simply haven't thought it through. Thirty-five hundred dollars is a *lot* of money. And you have no way of knowing whether this organization is legitimate."

"We *want* to believe you when you say you know what you're doing, Jess," Mrs. Wakefield put in. "But it's very difficult for us to trust you when you can't even see how irresponsible your actions are. Depositing that money without asking us was *not* a mature and independent thing to do."

"You're so unfair!" Jessica cried. "It's fine for *Liz* to go off to New York City for the summer because *she's* Miss Goody Two-shoes, but *I* can't go to Florida because *I'm* the *evil* twin. Well, I'm going, and you . . . can't . . ."

It took Jessica a few seconds to realize she'd said something terribly wrong. Obviously she had because the faces of Ned and Alice Wakefield were rapidly turning into something resembling livid, wide-eyed pickled beets.

"Elizabeth is going *where?*" they bellowed in unison.

"Thanks so much for tonight, Tom," Elizabeth said with a quick smile as she fished her keys out of

43

her handbag. "I really enjoyed the carnival. I felt like a kid again."

*Was there a strained note in her voice, or am I just being paranoid?* Tom wondered. In the dim glow of the light over the Wakefields' front door, Elizabeth's face was unreadable.

Tom reached out, tucked a lock of Elizabeth's hair behind her ear, and looked intently into her eyes. "I *always* have a great time when we're together," he said softly. "Liz, please, just remember how much I'll miss you if you go. That's all I ask."

*Did that sound too manipulative?* Tom wondered as he studied Elizabeth's expression. Her blue-green eyes reflected a shifting sea of emotions. She glanced away, looking almost pained.

"I will, Tom," Elizabeth said thickly, her eyes trained on some point between his second and third shirt buttons. "I should be getting inside, OK? I'll call you tomorrow."

"I'll be waiting," Tom vowed. "Good night, Liz."

Part of him longed to sweep her into his arms and kiss her so passionately she'd be too weak to board a plane. But tonight Tom knew he'd be better off keeping his distance. He contented himself with planting a soft, lingering kiss on her cheek before she murmured her good night and turned to unlock the door.

Tom trudged back to his car. As he slid into the driver's seat he saw Elizabeth disappear into the Wakefield house.

Cursing under his breath, Tom brought his fists down on the steering wheel in frustration. Then he dropped his face into his hands. "Get a grip, Watts," he mumbled. "You're acting like a total loser."

As Tom started the car all the petty, obnoxious things he'd said to Elizabeth echoed in his mind. *What was I* thinking? he berated himself. *Liz is obviously right—this fellowship is a huge honor, and only a pathetic, selfish* jerk *would try to hold her back*.

But as much as he hated to admit it, Tom knew exactly why he'd acted that way. And while he wasn't proud of his behavior, he knew he'd repeat it in a second if he thought there was even a slim chance Elizabeth would stay in Sweet Valley. The truth was, he just couldn't make it through the summer without her.

"Well, how nice of you to join us, Elizabeth," Mrs. Wakefield said in a voice thick with sarcasm. "I don't suppose you have any news you'd like to share?"

Elizabeth froze with her hand on the doorknob. Something was *very* wrong in the Wakefield house. Her parents were standing five feet from the open doorway, forming a barricade. Her mother's hands were on her hips, and her father's arms were folded sternly across his chest. In the living room Jessica sat huddled up on the couch, biting her nails anxiously.

"Hi, Mom . . . Dad . . . Jess," Elizabeth said

hesitantly, closing the door behind her. "Is something up?"

"Why don't you tell *us*, Elizabeth?" Mr. Wakefield countered. "Or is New York supposed to be some big secret?"

Elizabeth whirled on her sister. "Jessica!" she cried accusingly. "You had no right to blab to Mom and Dad! I was going to talk to them once I made my decision!"

"I'm so supersorry," Jessica insisted, squirming. "It just kind of came out when we were talking about my plans."

"Your *plans*?" Elizabeth echoed incredulously. "You mean they're letting you go?" She jabbed an angry finger in her sister's direction. "Well, if *she* gets to go to Florida, then *I* should definitely—"

Jessica jumped to her feet. "Wait, that's not fair! You guys said *I* could—"

"All right, everybody, time-out!" Mr. Wakefield made a T sign with his hands. "Jessica, we never said you could definitely go. Elizabeth, we never said you definitely *couldn't*." He heaved a weary sigh. "Now, before we get too bent out of shape, why don't we all sit down and discuss this like mature adults."

Elizabeth and Jessica claimed the living-room couch while their parents faced them in armchairs.

"Girls, we know you're . . . well, we know you're not girls anymore," Mrs. Wakefield began. "You're young women. And we're proud of both of you for thinking about your future. Most college students just want to lie around on the beach

46

all summer, but you want to gain some valuable experiences. That's a parents' dream come true."

Mr. Wakefield nodded. "What we're *not* so thrilled about is the fact that you two were planning all this without talking to us first."

"But I just found out today!" Elizabeth and Jessica claimed in unison.

"I know, I know," Mr. Wakefield said tiredly. "But these are decisions that can't be made in one day. Both of you have a lot to think about first. That's why when Jess told us all this, we got so . . . so . . ."

"I believe the word she used was *ballistic*," Mrs. Wakefield supplied.

Mr. Wakefield leaned forward and fixed Elizabeth with a serious look. "Liz, we've already talked to Jess about why she shouldn't have taken money from this FSSA place. What about you? Have you thought about the cost of living in New York? Or if you can even afford it?"

Elizabeth swallowed hard. "Well, I've *thought* about it," she said sheepishly. "But I don't exactly know how to figure out the answers."

Mr. Wakefield leaned back in his chair and exhaled slowly while Elizabeth darted a glance at Jessica. She could actually feel the tension coming off her sister's body; she was coiled up like a spring.

Finally Mrs. Wakefield smiled. "OK, listen. We're not going to stand in the way of your goals. We'll do what we can to help. But *nobody* is leaving Sweet Valley unless your father and I are satisfied that you two are safe and provided for, financially and otherwise. Is that understood?"

"*Yes!*" the twins exclaimed together.

*I can't believe they came around so fast!* Elizabeth thought, exchanging a relieved look for Jessica's surprised one.

"What do we do now?" Jessica asked eagerly.

"Should I start looking for apartments tomorrow?" Elizabeth asked.

"I'm not so sure I like the idea of you living alone in New York City," Mr. Wakefield said, frowning. "There are a lot of creeps and sickos out there."

"I have a few college friends in the New York area," Mrs. Wakefield volunteered. "Maybe I could make a few calls and see if one of them can recommend a sublet or a share."

"That would be great, Mom!" Elizabeth exclaimed, feeling elated and nervous at the same time. Now that her parents were talking about New York as if it were a reality, it was starting to seem real to her too.

"And Jess, I'm going to look into this FSSA outfit and make sure they're on the level," Mr. Wakefield added sternly. "If anything sounds the least bit suspicious, you're going to return that money and find something else to do with your summer. Got that?"

"Yes!" Jessica clapped, jumped to her feet, and threw her arms around her father's neck. "Thanks, Dad!" she sang. "Thanks, Mom! You guys are the best. Liz and I are going to make you so glad you let us go. Right, Liz?"

"Right," Elizabeth confirmed weakly. Deep down she felt anything but sure of herself. Now that her parents were helping her, she had a real obligation to take the fellowship. Assuming everything panned out, she'd be on a plane to New York in less than a week. And in spite of her assurances to Tom, she hadn't even once reconsidered her decision to leave him behind.

# Chapter Five

"Would you care for another massage, Jessica?" Vince Klee murmured, his full lips trailing a delicious line along her deeply tanned collarbone. "Or could I perhaps refresh your mango smoothie? Anything for my sweet angel of mercy."

Jessica reclined farther back in her lounge chair and angled her body toward the blazing orange Miami sun. "Mmmm, that won't be necessary," she murmured sleepily. "I like you exactly where you are."

"No, please, my angel," Vince begged. He dropped to his knees beside Jessica's chair and gently took her hand between his. "If it weren't for your kick-boxing skills, I wouldn't be alive today. Let me do something for you."

"Well, if you insist, I guess you could rub my feet." Jessica yawned, lazily draping one bronzed calf over the side of her lounge chair. "But don't block my sun!"

Just then a shrill ring sliced the air.

*"Oh no—my cell phone!" Jessica shrieked, jumping up from the chair. "Someone's in trouble!" She dug frantically in the sand, but the cell phone was nowhere to be found. . . .*

Jessica sat up in bed with a start and fumbled for the jangling phone on her nightstand. "Hello?" she croaked into the receiver, her voice thick and blurred with sleep.

"Ms. Jessica Wakefield, please," a brisk male voice requested.

Jessica cleared her throat. "Uh, speaking. Who's calling, please?"

"Ms. Wakefield, this is Lieutenant Ron Gorman of the Florida Specialized Security Academy. On behalf of everyone here at FSSA, I'd like to welcome you aboard!"

"B-But how did you know I enrolled?" Jessica squeaked.

"You deposited the check, of course!" Lieutenant Gorman replied. "Congratulations, Private Wakefield. You're one of us now! It's an elite corps, but I know you've got what it takes. We expect to see you rough and ready, reporting for duty this Monday at oh-seven-hundred hours."

"But how do I *get* there?"

"You've got thirty-five hundred dollars in your bank account, remember?" Lieutenant Gorman chuckled. "We'll arrange to have someone meet you at the airport on Sunday. Just let us know which flight you're on. See you soon, Wakefield!"

Jessica exhaled deeply with relief as she hung up

the phone. *I practically forgot about that money!* she mused. *Well, after I buy my ticket, that'll leave me with about—*

"Oh no!" she croaked. "What about tuition? It's ten thousand dollars! Where am I going to get the rest of the money?"

Jessica stood up and paced her messy room. "OK, Wakefield," she muttered. "This is the moment of truth—the eleventh hour. What would James Bond do in this situation?"

She looked at the phone. "Call Daddy," she decided.


"Miller Huttleby Foundation. How may I help you this morning?"

"Er, hello, I'd like to talk to someone about accepting a fellowship," Elizabeth said as she nervously tapped her fingernails on the phone receiver. "With whom should I speak, please?"

"Well, I'm Althea Mason, director of admissions," the voice responded warmly. "And you must be Elizabeth Wakefield."

"How did you know?" Elizabeth asked, surprised.

"How many fellowships do you think we give out?" Ms. Mason replied with a silvery laugh. "Our other two recipients have already confirmed. That left only you, Elizabeth."

"Well, I'm really honored to have been accepted," Elizabeth said. "Now that I'm confirmed, is there anything I should know besides the information in the packet?"

"Just be at the airport on Sunday for your nine A.M. flight to La Guardia," Ms. Mason replied cheerfully. "Your first-class ticket will be waiting when you check in. And don't hesitate to call us if you have any other questions."

"That's all?"

"That's all."

"Wow—thanks so much! I'm really looking forward to the summer."

"So are we, Elizabeth. See you soon."

"Yes—good-bye." Elizabeth hung up the phone, glad that Ms. Mason couldn't see the silly grin that had spread across her face. *How lucky am I?* she exulted. *This summer is going to be unforgettable!*

A pang of wrenching guilt pushed her happiness aside. *How could I get so excited about abandoning Tom?* she asked herself. *And how could I make the decision so quickly?* Just knowing that Tom was sitting at work, blissfully unaware of her actions and still filled with hope, made her feel deceitful and ashamed. Summoning all her strength, she picked up the phone again and dialed.

"Action Five News."

"H-Hello," Elizabeth began mournfully. "I need to speak to Tom Watts, please. It's very important. . . ."

Tom scribbled a smiley face on his Action 5 News stationery pad and scratched it out so fiercely, the tip of his pencil shattered into dust. He loosened his fist, let the pencil fall, and dropped his head into his hands.

*Watts, you've really lost it,* he told himself mournfully. *Here you are, a college man on summer break. You have a cushy internship that any reporter worth his weight in office supplies would kill for. And how have you spent the past two hours? Doodling!*

Tom tore off the sheet of paper. *It's not my fault I can't concentrate,* he countered, angrily crushing the sheet into a ball. *How can I even* think *straight after Elizabeth dropped that bombshell on me?*

The truth was, it hadn't been much of a bombshell. Tom knew deep down that Elizabeth had already made up her mind; he just hadn't wanted to admit it. Now he wasn't feeling shocked, just sad. And hopelessly lonely, despite the fact that Elizabeth hadn't even left yet.

"It *is* a great opportunity for Liz," Tom admitted aloud, rolling the ball of paper between his hands. "I can't really blame her."

When she'd broken the news, he'd wanted to be angry or at the very least say something to make her feel guilty. But when Elizabeth broke down and sobbed that she was going to miss him desperately, Tom's heart had melted. He'd signed off then, telling her he had to get back to work, but the truth was that if he'd stayed on the phone any longer, *he'd* have started crying too.

Tom raised his arm and tossed the wadded-up paper toward the wastebasket on the far side of the office. He missed by a mile.

*Yesterday it seemed like everything was going my way,* he thought miserably. *Now it's like* nothing *is!* The internship that had made him feel like such a big man now seemed like just another summer job—something that was keeping him from spending as much precious time with Elizabeth as he could.

Tom stood up and looked around his office. Sunlight streamed through the window; a leafy potted plant sat on the sill. His desk was piled with videotapes, magazine clippings, and interview transcripts from the station's archives. *My office is perfect, and so is my job,* Tom acknowledged despondently. *But none of it means anything without Elizabeth. None of it.*

Tom got up, picked up the crumpled paper, and threw it away properly before walking out of his office. He didn't look back, even though part of him wanted to. Before he could stop himself, Tom was standing in the doorway to John McGowan's office.

Mr. McGowan looked up from his desk and smiled. "Hi, Tom. What can I do for you?"

Tom exhaled deeply. "This is probably the stupidest thing I've ever done in my life," he announced, "but I quit."

"I can't believe it's been five years since we all got together, Tish!" Mrs. Wakefield gushed, sounding for a split second like a giggly college girl. "You should *really* come back to Sweet Valley more often."

Elizabeth stole a glance over at her mother, who was cradling the cordless phone between her head and shoulder as she stirred spaghetti sauce. *Mom gets so giddy when she talks to her college friends,* Elizabeth thought affectionately as she chopped up a red pepper. *I can just imagine what she was like when she was eighteen too.*

Elizabeth hadn't seen her mother's old sorority sister Tish Ellenbogen since she was a toddler, but Mrs. Wakefield had told plenty of stories about their Theta days—organizing dances and pep rallies, designing homecoming floats, and staging elaborate pranks on pledges. Elizabeth knew that Tish was divorced, living in New York, and had two daughters in college; she called and wrote frequently and sent out the coolest Christmas cards.

"The kids are great, thanks—except they're not kids anymore," Mrs. Wakefield said with a laugh. "I love them with all my heart, but they make me feel so *old!*" She giggled again and sprinkled dried basil into the sauce. "Actually, Tish, the kids are the main reason I'm calling—well, Elizabeth in particular. . . ."

Feeling suddenly morose, Elizabeth gazed down at her pile of chopped peppers as Mrs. Wakefield explained the situation to her friend. *I should be so excited,* she reminded herself. But the closer New York came to being a reality, the more empty she felt. All she could think of was how much she would miss Tom.

"Uh-huh, uh-huh," Mrs. Wakefield was saying.

"For how long? Oh, my, that works out perfectly! Elizabeth will be so excited!" Mrs. Wakefield cupped her hand over the mouthpiece. "Great news, Liz!" she exclaimed. "Tish's daughters are both away for the summer. If you'd like to stay at her place on the Upper West Side, she'd love the company!"

Elizabeth forced a smile. "Wow, that sounds wonderful," she said politely, unable to match her mother's enthusiasm. "Please tell Tish I appreciate it."

Mrs. Wakefield took her hand off the mouthpiece. "Tish? Elizabeth accepts your offer. . . . Uh-huh, she's so excited. . . ."

*It's really going to happen*, Elizabeth told herself. *I have a place to stay. I'm going to New York!*

She tried to picture the Statue of Liberty, the Empire State Building, Times Square. But the image of Tom fastening the gold bangle around her wrist kept intruding in her mind.

When the doorbell rang, Elizabeth wiped her hands on a dish towel and went to answer it. As she left the kitchen she could hear her mother asking, "So, how many sweaters do you think she'll need?"

When she opened the front door, Elizabeth gasped. There stood Tom with his hands behind his back. He was wearing a navy blue suit, but the top button of his shirt was undone, and his tie was draped around his neck. Wordlessly he produced a gleaming red apple from behind his back and held it out to Elizabeth.

"Tom, how—what are you—" Elizabeth sputtered. "I mean, aren't you supposed to be at work?"

He flashed her a grin that was half sheepish, half mischievous. "I quit my internship," he admitted. "Here, this is for you." He stepped forward and pressed the apple into Elizabeth's hands. "I was going to get flowers, but this seemed more appropriate."

Elizabeth gazed at the apple uncomprehendingly.

"OK, so it was a pretty cheesy gesture," Tom conceded. "The Big Apple, get it?" He exhaled deeply. "Liz . . . what I'm trying to say is, I quit my internship because I realized that it was meaningless to me if I couldn't be with you. I'd like to go to New York too . . . if that's OK with you."

Tears sprang to Elizabeth's eyes. For a moment she was too overcome to speak; she felt as if she were melting. "OK?" Elizabeth finally whispered. "Tom, this is . . . this is the sweetest, most romantic thing anyone could ever do!" She threw her arms around his neck and felt his encircle her waist tightly. For a moment they clung to each other without speaking.

After a minute she lifted her tear-streaked face from Tom's neck and took a step back. "Are you really sure you want to do this?" she asked anxiously. "How are you going to support yourself?"

Tom took hold of one end of his tie and used it to dab away the tears on Elizabeth's face. "I'll find a job," he assured her. "New York City is full of 'em."

Elizabeth beamed, deeply touched by Tom's devotion. Then another worry seized her. "But where are you going to stay?"

Tom cleared his throat. "Well," he said slowly, "I was thinking . . . uh, maybe we'd get a place . . . together."

From the kitchen Elizabeth heard her mother practically scream with laughter, evidently at some joke she was sharing with Tish.

"Now, before you say anything, Liz, just hear me out," Tom went on hurriedly. "First of all, rent in New York is notoriously expensive, and it makes sense to look for a share. Second of all"—he drew her close, his voice dropping to a whisper—"I would never, *never* expect you to do anything you don't feel ready for. Just because I want to be close to you doesn't mean that I'd take advantage."

Elizabeth's mind was whirling. This was all too much to grasp at once. *It would be so much fun to live with Tom,* she mused, *but on the other hand, it might be dangerous. Tom says he won't pressure me, but what if I get tempted too?* Sometimes when he held her close enough to feel his breath on her ear, she felt as if—

"Liz, please say something. Can you trust me?"

Elizabeth met Tom's eyes. "Yes, but . . . I don't know if I trust *myself,* much less the two of us together. We might get tempted . . . and not be able to stop."

She shook her head in amazement at the ideas running through her brain. Despite what she'd just said, a tiny part of her couldn't help wondering: *If we did end up in bed, would that be so wrong?*

"Besides," Elizabeth continued with a sigh, "I already have a place to stay—"

"Oh, don't worry about a thing, kids."

Elizabeth jumped away from Tom and spun around to see her mother, still holding the cordless phone. *How long has she been standing there?* she wondered, her face flushing beet red.

"I already asked Tish, and she has room enough for *two* in her apartment." A smirk played at the corners of Mrs. Wakefield's lips. "Remember, Elizabeth, mothers know *everything.*"

"OK, Jessica." Ned Wakefield took off his glasses and rubbed his eyes. "I've checked out FSSA completely. By all accounts, they run a well-respected training program. Their claims about the average salaries of graduates check out. And they do have some bodyguards among their alumni."

Sitting on the couch across from her father, Jessica hugged her knees to her chest. "I knew it!" she crowed. "So I can go?"

"Not so fast," Mr. Wakefield said sternly. He leaned forward and picked up some papers from the coffee table. "I also did some research on their financial aid program. The money you received was a grant—you don't have to pay it back. But the rest of the tuition is *your* responsibility."

Jessica gulped and lowered her bare feet to the floor. "But I don't have that kind of money!"

"No, but you don't have to pay it all right

now," Mr. Wakefield explained. "The FSSA rep I spoke with looked up your file. You've been identified as a promising candidate—evidently the police academy forwarded your application with a recommendation."

Jessica beamed. *So at least the police academy* did *think I had potential,* she thought proudly.

"Anyway, they have a financial aid program," Mr. Wakefield continued, "so you would be able to pay back the sixty-five hundred in monthly installments over the next two years. Now that might mean a work-study job down the line, or—"

"Cool!" Unable to sit still any longer, Jessica leaped to her feet. "So *now* can I go?"

Her father sighed and leaned back in his chair. "Jessica, if you truly want to go, we'll do what we can to help you out financially. But you *will* incur some debt, so I suggest you read the payment plan agreement thoroughly before you decide." He held out the papers.

"Sure, Dad, I will," Jessica promised, grabbing the papers. She leaned over and planted a kiss on her father's cheek. "Thank you *sooo* much. You're the greatest dad in the world. I'm going to go upstairs and read these right now."

Jessica bounded up the stairs and into her room, slamming the door behind her. Once she was safely in her room, she tossed the papers onto her desk and jumped on her bed. *I'm going! I'm really going!* she cheered inwardly. *Who cares what those papers say? I'll have no problem paying back the money after I get a top secret job!*

She rolled off the bed, grabbed the blow dryer from her dresser, jumped back onto the bed, and aimed at the door. "Freeze, dirtbag!" she shouted in her most commanding voice.

Imagining that her tank top and shorts were a black spandex cat suit, Jessica spun around and executed a roundhouse kick. *"Hiii-ya!"* she cried. "You're dead meat now, buddy!"

Jessica fired off several imaginary rounds with the hair dryer, lifted it to her lips, and blew across it suavely. *I'm a natural,* she thought giddily. *FSSA is going to love me. From now on, my life is going to be just like an action movie!*

# Chapter Six

"I can't believe we're really on our way," Elizabeth said excitedly, squeezing Tom's hand. "Isn't it fun traveling first-class? I feel like a movie star."

She flashed Tom a giddy grin and turned to glance out the window. Outside the plane the California highways and palm trees receded to the size of a toy train set.

*I'm going to New York!* Elizabeth cheered silently, suppressing the urge to bounce up and down in her seat like a little kid. After all, *she* was supposed to be the levelheaded twin.

Already this morning Elizabeth had called ahead to confirm the flight to New York, checked off the last ten items on her packing checklist, and forced her chronically late sister to cut short her makeup regimen so they wouldn't miss their flights. By the time she and Tom checked in at the gate, Elizabeth felt as if every muscle in her body were strung taut. But now that she was sitting on the plane with her boyfriend beside her, with nothing else to plan, worry about, or double-check, Elizabeth was finally starting to relax.

"Tom? Don't you feel like a celebrity in these seats?" Elizabeth asked, eager for him to share her buoyant mood.

For a split second she thought his face looked almost stormy. "I *always* feel like a star when I have a gorgeous blond babe like you on my arm," Tom said, wiggling his eyebrows in a mock-studly manner.

Elizabeth giggled and punched Tom playfully on the arm. But she was watching his face closely. *Is he upset that things didn't work out the way he wanted?* she wondered anxiously. *I know he wasn't expecting our first shot at "living together" to include a chaperone.*

Sighing quietly, she turned back to the window. While helping Elizabeth plan for her trip, Mrs. Wakefield had told her many anecdotes about the "good clean fun" she and Tish had shared at Theta house and mentioned several times how incredibly relieved she was to know Tish would be "looking after" Elizabeth. After her mother stated repeatedly that under no circumstances would she have allowed Elizabeth to live with Tom unsupervised, Elizabeth had a pretty good idea of how Tish was supposed to "look after" her.

*I guess I'm glad Tish will be around to keep me from doing anything I might regret,* Elizabeth decided as she gazed at Tom's tanned, muscular arms. Under his white T-shirt she could see the outlines of his broad, well-defined chest muscles, evidence

66

of his days as an SVU football star. He was undeniably sexy. When she looked at Tom . . . when she thought of how he'd dropped everything to be with her . . . it was hard to recall *what* she would regret if their relationship went to the next level.

*The truth is, I don't know what I'm missing,* Elizabeth admitted silently. *Tish might be looking out for me, but she could be keeping me from doing something I'd like . . . a lot.*

Tom's gaze met hers. "What?" he asked, a note of alarm in his voice. "Why are you looking at me like that?"

Elizabeth felt her face grow warm. "Like what?"

Tom shrugged. "I don't know. Like you're sizing me up."

Elizabeth bit her lip and smiled. "I was just thinking . . . that this summer is going to be quite an adventure."

*What does she mean by that?* Tom wondered as Elizabeth turned back toward the window. *Is she still upset because of the thing with the tickets? I can't help it if I can't make a habit of traveling first-class!*

At the ticket counter Tom had asked for a seat in coach, and Elizabeth had looked confused. "Don't you want to sit together?" she'd asked in a hurt tone. "My ticket's in first class, remember?"

Tom *didn't,* in fact, remember her ever saying that, but what could he do? Even though a last minute, first-class ticket was beyond pricey, it would have been an extremely lame move to ditch Elizabeth for the sake of saving a few bucks.

Still, he gulped when the ticket agent told him how much more first class cost. When he hesitated a moment, Elizabeth offered to exchange *her* ticket to be with him. Tom instantly felt like a royal jerk and bought a seat in first class.

*A few hundred bucks more for free headphones and an extra bag of peanuts,* Tom thought sourly. *And Elizabeth still seems like she's disappointed in me.*

"Tom?" Elizabeth suddenly turned around, as if she had heard his thoughts. "You're not . . . I mean . . ." Her aquamarine eyes searched his face intently. "You're looking forward to this as much as I am, right?"

Tom smiled with relief. *I was just getting uptight over nothing,* he told himself. *Liz loves me—she doesn't care about bogus stuff like flying first-class.*

"Of course I am," Tom assured her earnestly. "I still can't believe we're going to live together—I keep thinking your dad is going to wake up, realize what he agreed to, and fly east to break my legs."

Elizabeth giggled. "It *is* pretty wild, isn't it?"

Tom grinned. Elizabeth looked so beautiful when she was laughing, her eyes sparkling with humor and happiness. Even in her SVU sweatshirt and jeans, with her blond hair pulled back in a loose ponytail, she was radiant. *It's going to be like heaven on earth to see Liz's face every morning when I get up and every night before I go to bed,* he marveled. *What difference does it make if I blew a few extra bucks? I'd pay any price to be with Liz.*

"Sir, another beverage?" A flight attendant in a crisp navy uniform had materialized out of nowhere in the aisle next to Tom, extending a tray of sodas.

"Yes, thank you," Tom responded automatically. "I'll have a root beer. And I'm guessing the lovely young lady on my left wants a diet soda."

"I can't get over this service!" Elizabeth exclaimed as the flight attendant placed drinks and freshly baked cookies on their seat-back trays. "It just feels so *decadent*, doesn't it?"

"Decadent . . . yeah," Tom echoed hollowly, his spirits dampened by the reminder that they were traveling in high style.

*If Liz is enjoying herself, that's what really counts,* Tom reminded himself as he popped the top of the root beer can. *I'd just better make sure I consume a few hundred dollars' worth of soda and cookies.*

"Excuse me . . . is this your magazine?"

Jessica turned—and stared. A tall young man with black hair and sideburns stood in the aisle of the airplane, pointing at the crumpled copy of *Ingenue*'s fall fashion preview she had tossed on the seat beside her. He carried a large duffel bag and was wearing a black cable knit sweater and camouflage cargo pants. Under the thick sweater his body appeared to be built like a brick wall—biceps swelled under his long sleeves, and his chest was impossibly broad. As his ice blue eyes gazed questioningly into hers, Jessica thanked her lucky stars that she'd managed to apply foundation, loose powder, and lip gloss before her hyperresponsible sister dragged her into the car.

"Excuse me," the hot guy repeated. "I think

this is my seat—16C. I don't want to ruin your magazine, so . . ."

"Oh, I'm so sorry!" Jessica cried, recovering from her paralysis. She snatched up her magazine and flashed the guy a dazzlingly apologetic smile. "I just spaced out for a second there. You know how, uh, flying . . . uh, airplanes do that to me sometimes." *Real slick, Wakefield*, she chastised herself mentally. *Why don't you just tell him you were picking your jaw up off the floor?*

A momentary look of confusion passed over the guy's face and was quickly replaced by an amused grin. "OK, whatever," he agreed as he took his seat. "I'm Harlan Edwards."

"Jessica Wakefield," Jessica replied with a sheepish smile. She took his hand and winced at the pressure of his grip. "It's nice to meet you, Harlan. Are you headed for Florida?"

"Yeah." Harlan released Jessica's hand. "This summer I'm training to be a special agent at the Florida Specialized Security Academy."

"No *way!*" Jessica sat bolt upright and clapped. "That's exactly where *I'm* going! We'll be training together!"

"Really? No kidding?" Harlan scanned Jessica with his blue eyes as if he were reassessing her. "Well, Jessica Wakefield, you must be one tough cookie under that fashion model exterior! What drew you to FSSA?"

Jessica looked down at her black stretch-velvet cat suit and thigh-high black leather boots. For once she *hadn't* been trying to look like a fashion model; she was going for the secret-agent look. "Actually I was planning on going to the police academy," she admitted. "But they were already full when I applied, so they passed on my application to FSSA with a recommendation. Now I'm thinking I may go into bodyguard work."

"I'm impressed," Harlan said, looking deeply into her eyes. "Beautiful *and* powerful. It'll be a pleasure training with you, Jessica."

Jessica was momentarily unable to breathe— Harlan's intense gaze held her transfixed. *Those are the kind of eyes a girl could get lost in,* she thought dreamily. But quickly she regained her composure and crossed her legs casually. "So, what about you, Harlan?"

"Well, being a special agent has always been one of my dreams, but there was so much I wanted to do first," Harlan explained, leaning back as the plane began to ascend. "I was in the Marines for a while. After I was discharged, I got my black belt in aikido and worked as a private bodyguard for a few months. I used to guard that actress India Jordan . . . heard of her?"

"*Heard* of her?" Jessica breathed. "I was just reading an interview with her." She pointed to the rumpled copy of *Ingenue* on her lap. "That must have been an *amazing* job!"

Harlan nodded, the corners of his mouth turning up with satisfaction. "I must have fought off photographers a million times. And once I managed to get a gun away from some loony fan right before it went off. We were arriving at a premiere,

71

and I spotted the guy in the crowd and kicked the gun out of his hand. Of course, there were dozens of photographers around, so my picture was all over the papers the next day. I felt pretty cool."

"*Pretty* cool? That's the coolest thing I've ever *heard!*" Jessica exclaimed. "It's like a scene right out of India's last movie, *Sustained Injury*. I must have watched it a million times, and you've *lived* it!"

Harlan beamed. "As a matter of fact, the director consulted with me before he shot that scene. But still, I'd have to say my all-time favorite is *Severe Disturbance*. The part where India swings from the chandelier while blowing away terrorists is just *awesome*."

Jessica's spirits soared as high as the plane. She could already picture what a butt-kicking team she and Harlan were going to make during training . . . and possibly in their *off* time too. Harlan didn't seem like the type to be fazed by working out all day and club hopping in Miami Beach all night. *I'll get him to show me some of his aikido moves,* Jessica resolved, *and to introduce me to some Hollywood types too. After that, who knows where our relationship could go?*

"Excuse me, please," Elizabeth panted as she staggered forward, her two heavy suitcases banging against her legs. "Excuse me—coming through."

The crowd of people surrounding the baggage carousel showed no indication of budging—except for a heavyset man who nearly knocked Elizabeth backward onto the conveyor belt. Elizabeth followed quickly behind him as he elbowed his way through the throng of people. When she emerged, Elizabeth let out her breath, set her bags down on the ground, and looked around wildly for Tom.

*"Liz! Over here!"*

Elizabeth wearily hoisted up her suitcases and headed toward her boyfriend, who was waving his arms wildly.

"Hey, watch it, blondie!" an angry voice with a thick New York accent bellowed. "Look where you're going with that crap!"

Elizabeth whirled around to see that she had smacked one of her suitcases into a burly, red-faced man with a thick mustache. "Oh—oh, I'm so sorry!" Elizabeth stammered, hastily lifting up her bags.

The man glared at her for a moment, glanced down at her chest, and stalked away muttering something about people from California being a waste of space.

Elizabeth looked down and realized she was wearing her sweatshirt emblazoned with the words *Sweet Valley University, California. It might as well say, Kick Me, I'm a Tourist!* Elizabeth thought, mortified.

Tom appeared by her side, holding his duffel bag. With his free hand he took one of her suitcases. "Why do women always have to pack so much *stuff?*" he joked as they headed toward the huge automatic doors under the Ground Transportation sign. "What's in here anyway, *bricks?*"

"Don't start with me right now, Tom," Elizabeth warned. "I just want to get away from this mob scene."

Tom whistled and shook his head. "Five minutes after we get off the plane and you're already acting like a real New Yorker."

Finally Elizabeth and Tom emerged from the terminal and collapsed into the back of a cab. Elizabeth read Tish's address off the piece of paper her mother had given her, and the cabbie took off with a screech.

Elizabeth dropped her head onto Tom's shoulder and let out a huge sigh. "Thank goodness we got out of that airport in one piece. I thought those people were going to tear us limb from limb."

Tom chuckled and planted an affectionate kiss on Elizabeth's hair. "Don't worry, sweetie. Soon we'll be home, safe and sound."

"Mmmm," Elizabeth sighed contentedly, snuggling closer to Tom. "That sounds nice. Maybe I'll take a nice warm bath, and then we can do a little sightseeing."

"Sounds perfect," Tom agreed. "I'm sure we'll both get a second wind after we get settled in."

Just then the driver swiveled his head around to face them. "Hey, you two are a real cute couple." He grinned crookedly, revealing a gold tooth. "This your first time in the city?"

Elizabeth sat up straight as a rod and looked out through the front windshield. The highway was whizzing by, cars weaving past them from either direction. "Um, shouldn't you be keeping your eyes on the road?"

The driver glanced over his shoulder at the road for a few seconds. "Ah, fuggedaboutit. I've been driving since noon yesterday, I been out to La Guardia so many times—fuggedaboutit. I know this road like it was my own mother."

Elizabeth and Tom exchanged worried looks.

"Uh, that's an awfully long shift," Tom said hesitantly. "Maybe you should get some rest."

The driver turned back to the highway just long enough to veer across two lanes of traffic. "See, my old lady threw me out the other day," he explained, swiveling around again, "so I've been too upset to do anything but drive, see? I just punched in at work and I ain't punched out since."

"Mm-hmm," Elizabeth responded through clenched teeth. She was beginning to feel sick to her stomach. Her eyes wandered to the license that was posted against the Plexiglas wall behind the cabbie's head. It certainly looked real enough. *How could this guy have gotten a license?* she wondered, aghast. *He's completely insane! He shouldn't be driving at all, much less for twenty-four hours straight!*

"Tom," Elizabeth whispered anxiously. "What should we *do?*"

Tom put a comforting arm around her shoulders and held her close. "Just hang in there, Liz," he murmured. "Look—there's the skyline. We'll be there soon."

Clinging close to Tom, Elizabeth gazed out the window to her left. A seemingly endless wall of skyscrapers bordered her view, tightly packed onto the narrow island of Manhattan. The skyline was exactly the way Elizabeth imagined the city itself to be: larger than life, but totally overwhelming.

*I'm so glad Tom is here with me,* Elizabeth realized, reaching for his free hand and entwining it with her own. *If I was alone, this city would probably eat me alive. With Tom all I have to do is relax and go with the flow.*

"Feeling better?" Tom whispered into her hair as the car lurched toward the Triborough Bridge exit.

Elizabeth lifted her face and managed a crooked smile. "Believe it or not, I think I'm starting to loosen up."

"See, whadd' I tell ya?" The driver swung around to face them, his gold tooth twinkling as he grinned. "You two make a real cute couple."

"Excuse me, please," Jessica said in her sweetest voice. "Would you by any chance be the FSSA representative?"

The uniformed, dark-sunglassed man stood out like a sore thumb from the sea of tuxedoed limo drivers milling around the baggage claim area. The man stiffly inclined his head and extended one hand palm up. "Let's see some ID," he said gruffly.

*This is so scary and official!* Jessica thought, thrilled, as she fished through her enormous carry-on bag for her wallet. *FSSA must have an amazing reputation if they have to be so security-conscious.*

The FSSA rep pushed his sunglasses up onto his forehead as he examined Harlan's and Jessica's driver's licenses. "OK," he said finally. "I'm your driver. The van's outside."

*I bet the van is really sleek and black and high-tech,* Jessica guessed as she and Harlan followed the driver out to the parking lot. *Maybe it even talks, like the car in that old show with the guy from* Baywatch!

But when they reached the vehicle, the floodlights of the underground parking lot revealed only an unmarked, dingy brown van. Jessica waited for the driver to take her bags, but he simply unlocked the sliding door and walked around to the other side of the van.

Jessica hefted her bags into the back of the van and climbed in. She looked around for a wall of flashing control panels designed for state-of-the-art bad-guy tracking, but all she saw was a plain old van interior with a worn tan carpet. Harlan had already claimed the shotgun seat up front, so Jessica saw no choice but to sit cross-legged on the floor, wedged between her luggage and a spare tire.

As they pulled out of the parking lot Jessica craned her head for a glimpse of Florida, but she couldn't see over the dashboard. "So," she called out, "how far is it to Miami?"

*"Miami?"* The driver tilted his head to stare at Jessica through the rearview mirror. "You've got to be kidding. We're talking panhandle here."

"We have to *panhandle?*"

Harlan and the driver exchanged amused looks. "He means the *Florida* panhandle, Jessica," Harlan explained. "Picture the shape of the state."

Jessica blinked again. Geography had never been one of her favorite subjects. Who needed to

77

memorize maps when the world was full of hot guys who loved giving directions?

"We're going *north*, not south," the driver said with an exasperated sigh. "FSSA's nowhere near Miami—I don't know where you got that idea."

"The brochures said . . . ," Jessica began, then trailed off. Come to think of it, she *didn't* really recall reading anything about Miami. Maybe she'd just *assumed* it. What else *was* there in Florida anyway?

*It must be someplace really remote and secure and top secret,* Jessica thought. *I bet that's why the brochures never mentioned it.* She pictured lush stretches of unspoiled coastline dotted with wildflowers and deserted beaches with soft white sand where she'd stroll barefoot with Harlan under a glittering canopy of stars.

*This just keeps getting better and better!* Jessica thought, hugging her arms to her chest as the van rumbled on. *First Harlan, now a fabulously exotic location. I can't wait till we get there!*

# Chapter Seven

"OK, people, here ya go!" the cabbie shouted as he brought the taxi to a screeching halt. "Riverside Drive. Now you two cute kids have a real nice day."

Elizabeth and Tom quickly slid out of the cab as the driver went around to the back for their luggage. Elizabeth clutched Tom's arm as he counted out his cash.

"You can keep the change if you promise me one thing," Tom said as he extended the money. "Go get some sleep, OK?"

The cabbie winked, got back into the taxi, and sped away.

Elizabeth picked up one of her suitcases and teetered toward the apartment building on wobbly legs. "I wasn't sure if I'd ever feel the ground beneath my feet again," she said shakily. "That guy would never be allowed to have a license in California."

"Oh, come on, Liz," Tom said with a chuckle as he hauled the other two suitcases. "It wasn't *that* different from California. He *did* tell us to have a nice day."

"I'm not even going to respond to that." She set down her suitcase at the door of Tish's building and pressed the buzzer for 12C, then glanced around her, taking in the neighborhood. Riverside Drive appeared to be a wide, well-kept street of relatively small apartment buildings on the Upper West Side of Manhattan. It overlooked a park and, beyond that, the Hudson River.

Tish buzzed them in without a word, and they hurried through two sets of doors into the lobby. The elevator was tiny and old-fashioned, and Elizabeth had to hold her suitcase to her chest while Tom pulled the accordion door closed. Just as they tumbled out into the twelfth-floor hallway, a door down the hall flew open.

"Elizabeth, darling, is that you?" a voice called warmly. "Come *in*, come in! It's so marvelous to see you!"

Elizabeth turned to see Tish Ellenbogen approaching with her arms extended wide. Her salt-and-pepper hair was piled in a loose bun on top of her head. Large turquoise-and-silver earrings dangled from her ears, and several crystals hung from black cords around her neck. She was wearing a green crocheted vest with floor-length fringe over a flowing, diaphanous purple-and-gold blouse and a black peasant skirt. If not for her graying hair and the crinkle of laugh lines around her eyes, Elizabeth would have guessed her to be in her early thirties.

"Hi, Ms. Ellenbogen, it's so nice to see you

again!" Elizabeth exclaimed with what little energy she had left.

Tish waved her hand, and her silver bracelets jangled. "Please, call me Tish—I'm not hung up on that formal stuff. And this must be Tom! What a handsome young man." She swept Elizabeth and Tom into her arms for a hug before jumping back with a look of concern. "Oh, I'm picking up on so much stress from your auras!" Tish exclaimed. "Come inside, quickly!"

She hustled Elizabeth and Tom inside her apartment and disappeared around a corner, leaving them gaping in the doorway. Tish's corner apartment had one huge, high-ceilinged, L-shaped main room. The two outer walls were lined by picture windows that looked out over the drive and the park; the other side of the room held a plush couch and armchairs and towering, full bookshelves. Oriental rugs were scattered across the finished wood floors, and a wide array of stone, metal, and wooden statues—many, it seemed, of goddesses from different cultures—stood in corners or on mantels. The dining-room table was covered with candles and incense burners.

"Wow." Tom whistled as he gazed up at the enormous white paper lantern that hung from the ceiling. "This place is amazing."

Tish returned, carrying a white ceramic bowl. "Here we go," she trilled, setting it on the marble-top coffee table. "I could tell you had a rough trip, and I just had to stew some coriander for you. I find it's the most effective aroma for revitalizing and restoring energy when you're really drained." Tish plopped herself down on the couch with a contented sigh and smiled. "Please, kids, sit down—you must be exhausted!"

Elizabeth lowered herself into one of the armchairs flanking the couch, and Tom took the one on the other side. "Coriander?" she repeated. "I don't get it. How does that work?"

"Aromatherapy, my dear," Tish answered. "Didn't Alice tell you? Oh, well, I don't think she really 'gets' what I do either. I'm an aromatherapist—I use scents and natural essences to heal and release tension. I dabble in homeopathic herbs a bit too, but aromatherapy is really my calling. It's quite an amazing science."

"It *sounds* amazing," Elizabeth said politely, intrigued but unsure if Tish was a complete flake. "So how do you . . . treat people?"

"Well, first I find out a little something about my clients and figure out which kinds of vibrations they respond to," Tish explained, leaning back and lacing her fingers together. "For instance, I might ask for your star sign. Elizabeth, what sign are you?"

Elizabeth smiled. "Jess and I are Geminis, believe it or not."

Tish laughed. "Of course! The twins. You two are like two sides of the same coin. Night and day, right?"

Elizabeth nodded. "Exactly. We're complete opposites, but we couldn't be closer."

"For a Gemini," Tish declared, "I would recommend some rose oil to restore balance between the two sides of your personality or some apricot flower essence." Tish turned to Tom. "And what about you, dear?"

"Scorpio," Tom stated gravely. Elizabeth could tell from his dead-serious expression that he was trying hard not to laugh. "So, is there any hope for me?"

Tish reached over toward Elizabeth and squeezed her knee. "I'm proud of you, honey!" she declared, winking. "You picked a good one—handsome *and* a challenge."

Elizabeth laughed uneasily. "A challenge?" she echoed.

Tish nodded sagely. "This relationship represents a tremendous karmic challenge for you, Elizabeth. Geminis are very mental, very analytical . . . but Scorpios are very intense and passionate." She inclined her head approvingly at Tom, who grinned mischievously and waggled his eyebrows. "They're all or nothing. Not to mention *very* sexy. A great catch for a woman who isn't afraid of commitment. Are you into commitment, Elizabeth?"

"Um . . . yes, Tom and I . . . really love each other." Elizabeth's smile was tight, and she could feel her face turning pink. Out of all the possible scenarios she'd imagined, hearing her chaperone refer to her boyfriend as "sexy" had *not* been one of them.

"Well, that's wonderful," Tish said, smiling and clapping Tom on the shoulder. "I get a great vibe from you two. I can sense the coriander working, can't you? The impurities have definitely lifted from your auras. Why don't you get settled in while I make us all something to eat?" Tish got to her feet, then paused as if something had dawned on her. "Oh, I guess now is a good time to discuss our living arrangements for the summer. Will you two be sharing a room?"

Elizabeth's face felt as if it were on fire. She glanced over at Tom and was mortified to see him looking at her expectantly.

"N-No," Elizabeth squeaked. "No, we won't."

As soon as the words were out of her mouth, Elizabeth felt like a complete idiot. Tish looked almost as surprised by her answer as Elizabeth had been by the question.

"Well," Tish began, "why not?"

Elizabeth's jaw dropped. "I don't—we don't—I never . . ." She stared at Tom, hoping he would step in to assist her, but he just shrugged, the shadow of a grin tugging at his lips. It was obvious that he too was wondering *why not*. "We just . . . won't," she finished lamely.

Tish nodded slowly, as if she didn't quite understand.

*I guess Tish's pep rally days are far behind her,* Elizabeth realized. *It doesn't look like she's the chaperone type! If Tish isn't going to stop me from taking things further with Tom . . . will I have to stop myself?*

*Will I even want to?*

"This is absolutely delicious," Tom declared as he heaped a second helping of mixed beans and grains onto his plate. "How long have you been a vegetarian?"

"Oh, ten, fifteen years . . . who can count?" Tish pushed the bowl of mixed lettuces across the table. "Have some more salad, dear. See, I believe we get more energy from food that doesn't come from animals because the animals affect our karma. Elizabeth, more salad?"

"Sure, I'll have some more," Elizabeth replied. "You know, I agree with you about getting energy from vegetables, but I tend to chalk it up to vitamins, not karma."

Tom smiled as he watched Elizabeth ladle out salad. She had changed into a pearl gray sweater and leggings, and now she looked refreshed and relaxed. It would have been almost impossible *not* to relax—Tish's food was delicious, lit candles decorated the table, and the view of the sun setting over the river was spectacular.

*I think I'm going to like living here,* Tom decided contentedly. *Tish might be far out there, but her heart's in the right place. And this apartment is incredible!* He glanced again out the window. A luminous blue dusk was falling over Riverside Park; across the river the city lights of New Jersey twinkled.

"Well, darling, I don't think you have to worry about your karma," Tish assured her. "I can tell from your aura that you're a very innocent person. Very *pure*."

Elizabeth froze with a forkful of salad halfway to her mouth. Tom whisked his napkin off his lap and dabbed at his mouth to hide the sly smile that threatened to overtake his face.

"Oh, dear, I didn't mean it like *that!*" Tish hastily insisted. "I meant pure of spirit, not of body. Not that—not that there's anything at all *wrong* with making a decision to keep your body pure sexually. Men disturb your karma too, isn't that the truth?" She clapped Elizabeth on the shoulder and winked at Tom.

Elizabeth returned her fork to her plate, untouched. She plastered a tight smile on her face, but Tom could tell she was mortified.

"See, I don't like to judge people for the choices they make unless they're harming other living forces in the universe," Tish continued, clearly oblivious to Elizabeth's discomfort. "Myself, I believe in free love—I think it's fabulous that young people today aren't subjected to the same kind of repression that your mother and I faced. But hey, you kids aren't growing up in the same world. It's dangerous out there, especially for women. I respect anyone who chooses to protect herself and be safe." She nodded approvingly at Elizabeth. "It's really admirable to achieve that kind of self-control. But I don't think *I* could do it!"

Tom fought to keep from chuckling as Elizabeth squirmed in her seat. *How ironic is this?* he thought in amusement. *I was worried that Tish was going to cramp our style, but she's trying to get us to loosen up!*

Elizabeth suddenly flashed Tom a reproachful look, as if she knew what he was thinking. *Not that I would ever pressure Liz to do anything she doesn't want to do,* he amended guiltily. *I just want her to*

86

*keep an open mind. And it's nice to know Tish is open-minded too, so it won't be a big deal if Liz and I decide to share a room or . . . whatever.*

"You know, back in the days of the sexual revolution," Tish continued, "the dynamics between men and women were completely different." She paused, as if lost in thought. Tom glanced over at Elizabeth, who was pushing food around on her plate as if she was desperate to leave.

*OK, so it won't be a big deal to Tish,* he corrected himself. *But Elizabeth's about to combust!*

"Thanks again for this great dinner, Tish," Tom volunteered, hoping a change of subject would put Elizabeth at ease. "I actually feel up to sightseeing tonight—what do you say, Liz?"

"Sure, I'm up for it!" Elizabeth said brightly, her face awash with relief. "I have to start work at the theater tomorrow, so we should definitely see some sights now."

"Of course, of course!" Tish jumped to her feet and fluttered her arms. "Goodness, here I am rambling on, and you kids are anxious to see the city. Now are you sure you can find your way around by yourselves?"

"We'll be fine," Tom assured her, pushing back his chair. "Can we help you clean up?"

"Go, go!" Tish made shooing motions with her hands. "It's your first night in New York. Relax and have fun!"

Elizabeth stood up. "Thanks for dinner and for everything, Tish," she said. "I'm sure we won't be out late, so don't worry about us."

"Oh, I trust you!" Tish assured her. "Just be sure you take a cab home if it gets too late."

As they headed out the door Tom couldn't help smiling bemusedly. They had only been in New York a few hours, and already they'd been shaken up quite a bit—especially Elizabeth. *It'll certainly be interesting to see what* other *effects the city has on her,* he thought.

"Here we go," the driver grunted.

The van came to a sudden halt, pitching Jessica backward onto the floor. Harlan and the driver both got out of the van.

Jessica stood up on shaky legs and noticed that a thick rain was beating down on the windshield. *So much for my velvet outfit,* Jessica lamented, stooping to pick up her bags.

When she got outside, Harlan and the driver had already disappeared. Jessica squinted to see through the rain, but all she could make out beyond the parking lot were the faint outlines of a few clustered buildings and swampland, gray and undifferentiated in the pouring rain. *I hope the beaches are within walking distance,* Jessica thought as she trudged through the mud. *Now how am I supposed to figure out where I'm going? There aren't any signposts or anything!*

Jessica slogged up and down the rows of bunkers, feeling the rain stream down her face and seep through her clothes and boots. Finally she found the building marked Women's Barracks and pushed open the door.

Inside was a long room with cinder block walls

and a cement floor lined with narrow iron bunk beds. Nobody else was inside. It wasn't exactly the luxury spa environment Jessica had hoped for, but at least it was dry.

As the rain drummed on the roof Jessica dragged her soaking wet bags to the other end of the room and found a bottom bunk that didn't look occupied.

Jessica plopped down on the bed and rummaged through her luggage for her makeup bag. She took out her compact and squinted in the mirror, assessing the weather damage to her face. Her hair was dripping wet and matted to her head; her makeup was in streaks. *Ugh—I'm a mess,* she thought. *I can't let anyone see me looking less like a glamorous secret agent and more like a drowned rat!*

Jessica whipped out her hairbrush, tamed her tangles with a few deft strokes, and spritzed her hair with styling hold. Next she brushed on some loose powder and streaked a little blush under her cheekbones. She was just about to apply lipstick when she suddenly became aware that she was being watched.

About two dozen women in black uniforms were standing around her bunk. All of them had athletic builds and carried themselves with a soldierlike swagger, their arms folded across their chests or their hands planted on their hips. And they *all* looked *distinctly* underwhelmed by Jessica.

Most of the women appeared to be Jessica's age or a few years older, and one woman in particular appeared, in Jessica's opinion, to *not* be aging gracefully. Her short-cropped haircut did nothing for her hard jawline and narrow, lined eyes, and her thin lips were set in a contemptuous line. She seemed to be the leader of the group; the rest of the women kept a respectful distance from her.

"Well, well, well," the woman sneered, pinching her face so that the lines around her eyes stood out like ridges. "Good afternoon, princess. Sergeant Vanessa T. Pruitt—I'm *so* glad you could join us. Private Jessica Wakefield, I assume?"

"Y-Yes," Jessica stammered. "How did you know?"

"Everyone else has already arrived," Pruitt said with a withered laugh. "Too bad you decided to show up fashionably late—you just missed lunch."

"S-Sorry," Jessica mumbled, replacing the cap on her lipstick and tossing it back into her makeup bag. "I got here as fast as I could."

"Let me give you a word of advice, Princess Wakefield," Sergeant Pruitt said in a voice dripping with sarcasm. "If you want to make it here, you'd better put away your makeup and your attitude. This is a hard-core training program, not a fashion show. I don't know how a little prom queen like you ended up here, but you're going to have to pull your weight. Is that clear?"

"It's clear, but it's not fair!" Jessica cried indignantly, jumping to her feet. "I'm fully qualified to be here, and I'm *going* to pull my weight! How can you pass judgment on me for . . . for freshening up?"

Sergeant Pruitt snorted. "You'd better watch that smart mouth of yours, or you're going to end up in a lot of trouble. Believe me, I'll be keeping an eye on you. *Princess.*" She turned back to the group. "All right, everybody, listen up. I don't want any prima donnas on my squad. And I don't want *anyone* defying my authority. Is that clear?"

"Yes, sir!" the cluster of women chanted.

"Good." Pruitt glared at Jessica, her small brown eyes glittering with contempt. "I hope *everyone* here takes me *very* seriously." Turning to face the rest of the women, she clapped abruptly. "Dinner is at six sharp. Afterward there will be an orientation meeting in the main bunker. Until then unpack and enjoy your free time—it may be the last you get while you're here."

As Pruitt strode briskly out of the hall the women turned their backs on Jessica and began scattering to their bunks. Jessica heard a couple of them giggle.

One freckled redhead came toward Jessica, who smiled and opened her mouth to speak. As the redhead approached Jessica's bunk she swung herself lightly onto the ladder and up to the top bunk without acknowledging Jessica's presence. Jessica clamped her mouth shut, embarrassed even though no one appeared to have noticed.

*I guess nobody wants to deal with me now that I'm on Sergeant Pruneface's bad side,* Jessica figured as she flopped down onto her bunk. *Why did she have to single me out like that?*

Around her the other women were noisily joking, laughing, and shoving trunks under their beds. Jessica watched them out of the corner of her eye and wondered what to do. She wasn't used to

91

feeling so out of place; usually her sense of style worked in her favor when she was meeting new people.

*I can't let that dried-up little witch ruin my chance to fit in here,* Jessica decided, sitting up on her bunk. *I'll just use my natural charms and get these girls to loosen up.*

"So," she called up cheerfully to her bunk mate. "Where are you from?"

There was no response from the top bunk. Then after a moment a cloud of foul-smelling smoke wafted out into the air above Jessica's bed. A slender, freckled hand extended out above the top bunk . . . holding a fat brown cigar between its thumb and forefinger.

Jessica's jaw dropped. As she stared disbelievingly her bunk mate's finger tapped the cigar, sending a fine mist of ash fluttering down onto Jessica's luggage.

*What kind of place* is *this?* Jessica wondered anxiously. *It isn't like a glamorous action movie at all. It's more like one of those boring, depressing war films!*

# Chapter Eight

"Tom, it's so beautiful," Elizabeth breathed, almost reverently. She leaned forward, gripping the rails so tightly that her knuckles were white. "I feel like we're on top of the world!"

Tom nodded silently, drinking in the panorama beneath them. Except for an elderly couple several yards away, Tom and Elizabeth were alone on the observation deck of the Empire State Building. Under the clear night sky they could see the entire city: a blanket of glittering lights. Around the island of Manhattan the twinkling lights of bridges arced and dipped like decorations strung on a Christmas tree. Everything about the scene—the lights, the balmy night air, the strange stillness of looking down on the world—felt magical.

"It *is* pretty amazing," Tom agreed. "The whole city seems to move at such a frantic pace . . . but when you're up here, it kind of puts everything into perspective."

Elizabeth turned to him, her expression suddenly intent. "I was thinking the same thing," she murmured. "Well, not in those words exactly, but . . . I know what you mean. All my worries seem so small right now."

Tom put his arm around her shoulders. "Are you OK?" he asked. "I know today has been, well, quite an experience. At Tish's you seemed a little . . . stressed out."

Elizabeth glanced away for a second, then turned back and smiled. "I'm fine," she assured him, shaking her head. "I admit I had one or two little attacks of culture shock earlier. But now that I've had some time to think, I'm realizing that the whole point of coming here was to do something new and different. So I'm just going to try to be open to new experiences and . . . and not let my fears get in the way." She turned to gaze over the railing, seemingly lost in thought.

Tom watched Elizabeth's face closely as she scanned the horizon. Her golden hair whipped around her head in the breeze, and her cheeks were pink in the night air. She looked radiantly beautiful; despite the spectacular view from the observation deck Tom couldn't tear his eyes from her face.

*New experiences?* The phrase echoed in Tom's mind. *Is she talking about touring the city or . . . about us?*

"Well, Liz," he began carefully, "I want you to know that I'm behind you a hundred percent. I want to make this a summer we'll never forget. So whatever you want to do, or see . . . or try . . . while we're here,

I'll support you. Even if—if you decide *against* doing something or if you do have . . . fears . . . well, I'll support you then too. I don't want you to do anything you're not comfortable with just because you feel obligated to try it while we're here."

Elizabeth's aquamarine eyes gazed into Tom's. "Do you really mean that?" she asked in a low, urgent voice. "Because it means a lot to me to know you feel that way."

Tom nodded solemnly. "Whatever you want to do, I want to be there with you. And whatever you *don't* want, I don't want."

"But what if you *do* want something I don't want?" Elizabeth asked softly, her brow creased.

There was no doubt in Tom's mind as to what they were really discussing now. Still, he wished he knew what was going through Elizabeth's mind. Back at Tish's she'd seemed so rattled at the mere mention of sex that Tom had more or less resigned himself to the prospect of sleeping alone for the summer. But now she was practically promising to keep an open mind about it. And if her mind was open, then she was certainly open to suggestion. *I'd better watch what I say very closely,* Tom reminded himself.

"It doesn't matter," he assured Elizabeth, rubbing her shoulder affectionately. "There's nothing I could possibly want that would be more important than taking care of your needs."

Elizabeth smiled, relief and gratitude written plainly on her face. "I'm glad to hear that, Tom, but the truth is, I don't know what I need . . . or want." She shook her head. "I don't know how I feel about anything anymore. Just being here for a day has made me feel totally turned around, you know?"

Tom nodded. "I know. But don't worry about it—we've barely moved in. Let's just take things as they come."

Elizabeth leaned forward and planted a soft kiss on Tom's lips. "Thank you," she whispered. "For being such a supportive, caring boyfriend. I love you so much, Tom."

"I love you too, Liz. Madly."

As Tom drew her close and wrapped his arms tightly around her waist he could feel Elizabeth's heart thumping against his chest. *The city's really getting to Liz!* he reflected, almost reeling as he replayed their conversation in his mind. *Back in Sweet Valley she was totally inflexible on the subject of sex. And now . . . now it looks like she's really wavering. Maybe she'll come around to my way of thinking after all!*

Jessica rolled over onto her side and pulled the thin wool blanket tighter around her shoulders. The cold night air had seeped through the walls, and the blanket was totally inadequate. Furthermore, it smelled musty and was *khaki,* a color Jessica would never, under any circumstances, have used for a bedroom set. Between the cold, the sounds of wind and rain thrashing on the roof, and the mattress springs that kept poking into her back, Jessica had been lying awake in her narrow bunk for what seemed like hours.

*I can't even believe they expect us to get up at* six *tomorrow morning after a night on one of these torture devices,* Jessica thought in frustration, thinking back to the dire pronouncement on hours that Sergeant Pruitt had made earlier. *The dark circles under my eyes are going to be horrific. And after today, there's no way I can get away with using my cucumber mask to minimize them!*

Thunder and wind made loud roaring sounds outside. Across the room someone coughed. Jessica sighed and flopped onto her back.

*Up at six, lights-out at ten, no leaving the FSSA grounds,* she thought miserably, reviewing the low points of Pruitt's list of rules and regulations in her mind. *Even if there* are *beaches and nightclubs around here, I'm not allowed anywhere near them! Could it be that I'm actually about to experience a summer with no partying whatsoever?*

As thunder crashed outside the barracks Jessica reminded herself that she had Harlan to hang out with. And once her bunk mates saw her with a hunk like him, they'd definitely be impressed. She'd make friends soon enough. *Anyway, it doesn't matter whether I have fun while I'm here,* Jessica reasoned. *My career as a bodyguard in Hollywood will make this summer worth my while a million times over!*

Suddenly the wind died down, and from outside there was a roaring noise that was definitely *not* thunder. Jessica's eyes snapped wide open, and her heartbeat accelerated to what felt like a thousand beats a minute.

*Did I imagine that?* she wondered in a panic. *If not, I really hope it was just my stomach grumbling because I passed up the mystery meat loaf at dinner!*

Just then there was another loud roar—this one sounding *too* close to the building. "What *is* that?" Jessica gasped out loud before she could stop herself.

There was a snort of sardonic laughter from somewhere in the darkness. "Just the alligators, *princess,*" a dry voice responded.

*Alligators?* Jessica shivered from her scalp to the tips of her toes, barely hearing the few scattered bursts of mocking laughter that echoed across the room. She burrowed as far as she could under the flimsy wool blanket. *What have I gotten myself into?*

"Did you see how many piercings that girl had?" Elizabeth whispered in horror. "Isn't that painful?"

Tom chuckled and glanced over his shoulder. "Just think, those are only the ones we can see," he pointed out.

Elizabeth made a face. "I don't want to think about it." She reached for Tom's hand and squeezed it as they continued walking down the street. "It must be obvious that we're tourists. Nobody else is batting an eye."

It was almost midnight, but the streets of the West Village were crowded with people, and Elizabeth couldn't stop staring. It was obvious that downtown Manhattan was just as wild and eclectic as it was reputed to be. Already she'd seen a man strolling down the street with a python around his neck, a trio of black-leather-clad teenagers with gravity-defying spikes of green hair, and a bombshell in a white sequined gown who was six-foot five in heels and had an enormous Adam's apple.

"Want to stop for a cup of coffee?" Tom suggested as they passed a café with an outdoor terrace. The round white tables for two looked quaint and romantic, but Elizabeth shook her head reflexively.

"I have to be up early to get to the theater. If I have any caffeine now, I'll be up all night." The second the words were out of her mouth, Elizabeth felt foolish. The New Yorkers strolling the sidewalks and seated at outdoor cafés around her didn't appear to be worried about staying out past their bedtimes.

Looking around at the sophisticated downtowners, Elizabeth felt as if she'd lived a totally boring and sheltered life. All the other young couples appeared to be having animated discussions about art or politics and they had no apparent reservations about public displays of affection. The men were in black turtlenecks or artfully grungy jackets and jeans. The women were impossibly long legged, with a sleek European look. Elizabeth glanced down at her sweater and leggings and felt sure she stuck out like a sore thumb.

"Hey, speaking of painful fashion statements, look up ahead," Tom said quietly, pointing out a man whose bare back was covered entirely in tattoos and who was passionately kissing a woman with equally tattooed arms.

"Wow," Elizabeth said with a little laugh. "What

do you say—should we go get matching tattoos, Tom?"

"Sounds good to me." Tom pulled Elizabeth close and nuzzled her neck, sending a thrill through her body. "That's what I love about you, Liz—you're a true romantic."

Elizabeth giggled. As they passed by the tattooed couple she couldn't help taking one last sidelong look. They were clinging to each other as if the world were about to end.

*Everyone here is such an individual,* she mused. *Nobody seems to care what anyone else thinks—they just do what they feel like.* Compared to the people around her, Elizabeth felt like a young, naive, uncool prude. Her embarrassment at Tish's questions about sex seemed to belong in a different world. *I'm sure none of these couples needs their parents' permission or a chaperone to live together. And I bet they don't sleep in different rooms!*

As they passed by a row of boutiques Elizabeth caught sight of her and Tom's reflection in the glass storefronts. To her surprise, they didn't look much younger than the couples around them. At SVU she thought of herself and Tom as students. *But away from school we look more like . . . adults,* she realized. *And basically we are. We're totally independent—it's not like Tish is much of a chaperone!*

Elizabeth tilted her face to gaze searchingly at Tom's gorgeous profile. *Tom's the perfect guy—I can't imagine wanting to be with anyone but him,* she reflected. *After all, he followed me all the way across the country!*

She took a deep breath. *Why not?* she asked herself. *Lots of other couples our age don't think twice about having sex. Tom and I are committed, and we're adults. Why* shouldn't *we have an adult relationship?*

Elizabeth stopped in her tracks, tugging Tom's hand so that he stopped with her.

"What's up, Liz?" Tom asked.

"Tom," Elizabeth began breathily, feeling her body quiver, "I'm ready."

Tom furrowed his brow. "You're ready to go home? You want me to call a cab?"

"Well, yes, but . . ." Elizabeth bit her lip and turned her eyes down coyly. "I mean I'm . . . *ready.* Tonight."

Tom felt his jaw drop open as understanding dawned on him. Then he sprang into action, practically dragging Elizabeth by her hand to the curb. "Taxi!" he hollered. *"Taxi!"*

They only had to wait a minute or so for an empty cab, but to Tom it felt like the longest minute of his life. His mouth was dry, and his knees were shaking. He'd never imagined this moment would happen so soon, and now he worried that if there were one second's delay, Elizabeth might change her mind.

They slid into the backseat of the cab, and Tom gave the driver Tish's address. Before he had finished speaking, Elizabeth was running her fingers through his hair and pulling his face toward hers.

As the cab screeched into motion, Tom's lips found Elizabeth's. He kissed her passionately, with all the pent-up yearning he usually tried hard to hold back. It was unimaginably wonderful to know that for once he *wouldn't* be going back to his room alone and frustrated.

His hands ran down her arms, around her waist, and up the back of her sweater. Elizabeth shivered, and for a second Tom was afraid she was going to push him away. Then she sighed and seemed to melt against his chest.

The cab suddenly veered to the right, sending Tom flying to one side of the cab. A second later Elizabeth slammed into him, landing practically on top of him.

"Well, hello there," Tom said with a chuckle as he gazed at Elizabeth's face. "I didn't expect to see *you* here."

Elizabeth giggled giddily and flung her arms around Tom's neck. "Kiss me, you fool," she ordered, pressing her body even closer against his. The temperature in the cab seemed to be about a hundred and ten degrees.

*I feel like I've died and gone to heaven,* Tom reflected as they dissolved into another urgent, searching kiss. *And we're not even home yet!*

"Oh, Tom," Elizabeth gasped when they sat up and pulled apart for air. "I've never felt this way before!"

Tom gazed at Elizabeth, momentarily unable to speak. Her eyes were shining, her hair was tousled, and her face was flushed. Tom didn't think he had ever seen a more beautiful sight.

"Remember, this is just the beginning," he murmured, tracing the contours of her kiss-stung lips with his fingertip. "It's going to get even better." He cupped Elizabeth's face in his hands and pulled her toward him.

Just then the cab struck a pothole while moving at high speed. Tom felt his head bump the roof of the cab— *hard*. "Ow!" he and Elizabeth exclaimed simultaneously. Both rubbing their heads, they exchanged surprised looks and collapsed into laughter.

"The potholes of love, I guess," Elizabeth said with a wry grin.

"I didn't think wearing 'protection' meant we needed hard hats," Tom quipped, glancing out the window. The highway was whizzing by at a mile a minute as the cab wove precariously between trucks and buses.

Elizabeth looked suddenly alarmed, as if something had just occurred to her. "Speaking of which—"

"Taken care of," Tom assured her hastily. "I know it's a sad case of wishful thinking, but I picked up some condoms before we left Sweet Valley . . . just in case."

Elizabeth beamed. "Tom, you think of everything." Then her smile turned devilish, and she punched him playfully on the arm. "Or maybe you only think of *one* thing."

"No argument there," Tom agreed cheerfully. "In fact, can you guess what I'm thinking about right now?"

"I have a pretty good idea," Elizabeth whispered, tilting her head back and closing her eyes.

Drawn irresistibly, Tom leaned toward her softly parted lips.

At that moment the cab rattled violently as it absorbed another pothole. Just as Tom's lips brushed against Elizabeth's the backseat jogged up and down, and Elizabeth brought down her teeth on Tom's lower lip.

Elizabeth yelped. "Oh, sweetheart, I'm sorry!" she shrieked as she pulled away. The color drained from her face. "Tom, you're *bleeding!*"

Tom gingerly touched his fingertips to his lip and saw that they were dotted with red. "Oh, brother," he muttered, the force of his desire disappearing like a cloud of smoke.

"Hold still." Elizabeth inhaled sharply as she scrutinized his lip. "Hang on, I think I have a tissue here somewhere." She reached for her purse on the seat beside her and began rummaging through it.

"It *does* kind of sting," Tom admitted, hoping against hope that he'd be able to parlay Elizabeth's nursemaid instincts into rekindling the sparks of passion. Even though he was feeling more foolish than amorous, he couldn't yet accept the fact that his chance to make love to Elizabeth had just vanished in the blink of an eye.

"You kids a'right back dere?" The cabbie, a balding middle-aged man with a thick Brooklyn accent, swiveled his head around, extinguishing the last of the romantic mood like a bucket of cold water. "Sorry 'bout dat. Freakin' West Side Highway is a pile a crap, excuse my French. I dunno why dey don't fix dat pile-a-crap road."

"Please, just try to slow down enough to get us home in one piece," Tom said through clenched teeth.

As the driver turned back to the wheel Elizabeth produced a crumpled Kleenex from her purse and began dabbing frantically at Tom's lower lip. "Relax, honey," she urged in a soothing voice. "We'll be there soon. Look, we're already at Seventy-second Street."

*Maybe when we get home and clean up this cut, we can chill for a while and pick up where we left off,* Tom prayed, settling back against the seat with a sigh.

But when they opened the door to the apartment on Riverside Drive, they found Tish on the floor of the living room in her silk robe and pajamas, sitting cross-legged with her eyes closed. As Tom and Elizabeth burst in, Tish's eyes snapped wide open, and her expression changed from one of peaceful calm to one of alarm.

"Tom, you're hurt!" she cried, untangling her legs and scrambling to her feet. "Oh, you poor dear . . . just wait one second."

Tish dashed to the bathroom and returned bearing a large first aid kit, which she proceeded to dump out onto the floor. "I *knew* I was picking up on some kind of disturbance in my vibrations!" she exclaimed. "I couldn't sleep—that's why I came out here to meditate. I must have subconsciously *known* you needed my help!"

Tom's shoulders slumped in defeat as Tish descended on him with a bottle of witch hazel and some cotton pads. *Face it, Watts,* he told himself glumly. *You just lost your chance.*

Elizabeth pulled her white cotton baby tee over her head and slipped on a pair of plaid boxer shorts. Grabbing her hairbrush off the top of the dresser, she surveyed herself in the bedroom mirror.

"What were you *thinking?*" she demanded of her reflection as she tugged the brush through her tangled hair. Now that she was alone in her room, she couldn't help but feel relieved that she and Tom hadn't followed through on her impulsive decision.

*I've always vowed that I would never rush into sex because of a momentary urge,* Elizabeth chided herself as she got into bed. *And just look at me tonight—I didn't even* think *about protection until Tom brought it up! That was totally* not *a responsible way to start an adult relationship.*

She sighed and pulled the covers up around her, feeling immature and confused. Just as she was about to turn out the lamp on her nightstand, there was a knock at the door.

"Liz?" Tom's muffled voice called. "Can I come in?"

"Sure," Elizabeth responded. "It's open."

The door opened and Tom appeared, wearing his SVU Athletic Department T-shirt and a pair of navy blue sweats. There was a bandage on his cut lip. He grinned when he saw Elizabeth buried up to her chin in blankets.

"You look so cute," he said affectionately, taking

a seat at the foot of her bed. "Should I read you a story before I tuck you in?"

Elizabeth grimaced. "Thanks. Like I need to feel a little *more* infantile right now."

Tom laughed and rubbed her leg through the blankets. "Oh, Liz, don't feel bad. Tonight just wasn't our night. But the summer is young. We'll have other nights."

Elizabeth hesitated. Part of her wanted to throw herself into Tom's arms right then and there. But another part of her was beginning to worry that things were going too far *way* too fast.

"Tom, I love you, but it's been a really long day," she said with an apologetic smile. "I'll see you in the morning, OK?"

"OK. Good night, Liz." Tom stood up and bent to give Elizabeth a gentle, lingering kiss on her lips "No matter what happened—or didn't," he murmured, "I had an incredible time with you tonight."

For a moment Elizabeth couldn't breathe as she flashed back to their passionate cab ride. Under the blankets her hands unconsciously clenched fistfuls of cotton sheets. "Me too," she managed. "Good night, Tom."

Tom turned out the light and shut the door behind him. Elizabeth closed her eyes and savored the delicious tingle of his good-night kiss on her lips and the memory of his hands on her body. It was thrilling and terrifying at the same time to let herself feel everything Tom's touch had awakened in her.

*If any of the cabdrivers in New York were quali-fied or even* sane, *Tom and I would be making love right now*, Elizabeth realized with a shiver. *Reality check! Is that what I want to happen? My hormones definitely think so, but what about my* brain?

Elizabeth sighed and rolled over onto her side. It wasn't like there was *no* blood reaching her brain. She did have several solid, rational reasons for wanting to make love with Tom. *I love him, he loves me, I trust him, he's kind and understanding*, she ticked off in her mind. *And, of course, he gave up a plum job to move all the way across the country on a first-class flight he couldn't possibly afford . . . just to be with me. After going through all that to show that he loves me, will he really be willing to wait?* Elizabeth couldn't help wondering how kind and understanding Tom would be if she backed out now.

"Ohhh, enough!" Elizabeth groaned out loud. "I'm going to go insane if I keep worrying like this. And I've got an internship to start tomorrow!"

With that realization Elizabeth fought to push Tom—and sex—out of her mind. *As of tomorrow I'm actually directing an off-Broadway play*, she reminded herself. *I've never needed a good night's sleep more in my life!*

# Chapter Nine

"Summerti-i-ime, and the living's easy," Jessica trilled as she tucked the last stray lock of hair under her FSSA issue black cap. "The fish are—something . . . and it's OK to wear white shoes!"

She gave herself one last approving look in the bathroom mirror. Luckily the FSSA uniform was cut stylishly *and* did wonders for her figure. If Jessica had founded a cult of style, her first commandment would definitely have been, You can't go wrong with basic black.

Jessica turned and sauntered across the empty barracks, refusing to let her mood be dampened by the sheets of rain pounding against the windows. *Today's a new day,* she reminded herself. *I've got to keep my spirits up if I'm going to make up for my lousy first impression.*

Despite her resolve the sodden brown-and-gray compound that greeted her outside was definitely *not* a mood booster. Jessica surveyed the downpour for a second before ducking her head and dashing out into the rain. By the time she reached the mess hall, Jessica was uncomfortably aware that the rain had soaked through her uniform to her goose-pimpled skin. Still, she did her best to burst through the doors with a dazzling smile.

Scanning the room, she saw several long tables filled with young men and women in FSSA uniforms. Along the far wall was a buffet-style serving line manned by uniformed cadets. Jessica spotted her redheaded bunk mate sitting at the end of a table, flanked by an attractive, athletic African American girl with close-cropped, bleached-blond hair and a Filipina with sparkling eyes and long, unruly dark curls. As she glanced over at them Jessica was sure she caught them staring at her, and they quickly averted their eyes and huddled together in giggles.

"Oh, what*ever*. Get over it," Jessica grumbled as she headed for the breakfast line. While she held out her metal tray for a bowl of gluey gray oatmeal and a plateful of dried-out scrambled eggs, Jessica struggled to keep her ego from deflating. But as she turned away from the line Jessica found herself looking directly into the eyes of Sergeant Pruitt, who was seated at the front table . . . and fixing Jessica with a loathing, disgusted stare. Her eyes narrowed and glinting coldly, Pruitt seemed to be saying, *You don't belong here*.

Jessica cringed, feeling conspicuous as she hovered at the front of the room with her tray. Then she spotted Harlan waving to her from a table

110

toward the back. Immensely relieved, Jessica headed toward him, smiling brightly.

"Hey there!" Harlan greeted her, folding up his copy of *The Mercenary Times* as she set down her tray across from his. "How was your first night?"

"Uh, it was great," Jessica said hesitantly, taking an experimental spoonful of oatmeal. Harlan looked so powerful and hot in his uniform, like a real action hero, that she figured he wouldn't be impressed to hear how scared and alienated she'd felt.

"Mine too!" Harlan enthused, shoveling a forkful of egg into his mouth as he spoke. "I had an *awesome* time. I beat every guy in my barracks in the one-armed push-up contest. I can't wait until the formal competition starts, can you?"

"Competition?" Jessica almost choked on her oatmeal.

"Haven't you heard about the competition? Every exercise we compete in is worth points, and at the end of the summer the points are tallied to determine our class ranking. Of course, that rank is what gives you the edge for landing those special security jobs."

"Great," Jessica lied hollowly. "A little healthy competition sounds like fun." *I can't take the pressure!* her mind screamed. *Pruitt will be waiting for me to choke!*

"My sentiments exactly," Harlan agreed, a broad grin stretching his chiseled features. "It'll be a pleasure . . . *competing* with you, Jessica."

When a sharp whistle blast suddenly broke the air, Jessica's spoon clattered to the table. She looked up to see Sergeant Pruitt standing at the front of the room, one hand still on her whistle and the other resting on her hip.

"Listen up, people!" Pruitt barked, her wiry frame suddenly seeming to fill up the room. "In five minutes you will report outside the mess hall for your first training exercise—the obstacle course. Latecomers will be penalized five points."

"All right!" Harlan cheered. "Bring it on, baby!"

Jessica cringed. *An obstacle course? At* this *hour?* she thought, her heart sinking with dread.

"It's *very* easy," Tish assured Tom as she flipped a whole wheat blueberry pancake in a cast-iron pan. This morning her hair was hidden under a colorfully patterned cloth head wrap, and she was draped in a gauzy blue muumuu. A red rhinestone paste-on *bindi* dotted her forehead. "Just catch the downtown local on Broadway and get off at Thirty-fourth Street."

Tom nodded and circled the stop on his subway map. He put down his pencil and took another sip from his mug, wincing slightly as the hot coffee touched the healing cut on his lip.

"Can I look at that map for a second?" Elizabeth asked, pulling it across the table toward her. A lock of blond hair fell across her face as she bent to study the map, and Tom felt a surge of affection lift his heart. *Today's a new day,* he couldn't help thinking. *Maybe if I get this job, Liz and I can . . .* celebrate *later.*

After making a few calls based on ads he'd seen in

the *Times,* Tom had landed a noon interview at a small, independent TV production company. The guy on the phone had sounded extremely impressed with the resume Tom had faxed from Tish's study, and that good news put Tom in a confident, upbeat mood.

"OK, the first ones are ready!" Tish announced, holding up her spatula triumphantly. "Pass your plates!"

"Wow—this looks incredible!" Tom's mouth watered as Tish set a steaming stack of blueberry pancakes in front of him. He reached for the little metal pitcher of organic maple syrup. "Talk about royal treatment."

"They look delicious," Elizabeth chimed in. "Tish, I swear you're spoiling us."

Tish laughed as she plunked herself down across from Elizabeth and set her own plate of pancakes on the table. "I wish my *own* kids were as appreciative as you two," she said with a sigh. Her bracelets—today fat hammered-gold cuffs that reminded Tom of Wonder Woman—clanged together like pots and pans as Tish cut into her stack of pancakes.

Tom cut himself a bite of pancake, enjoying the quiet, domestic scene. Sitting across from Elizabeth at the breakfast table in his suit and tie, chewing a mouthful of pancake as he unfolded the sports section, Tom felt as if he'd transformed overnight from an immature college student into a *man*. Not only was he about to interview for a *real* job, he had a feeling his relationship with Elizabeth was about to become more adult as well. Coming to

New York was, without a doubt, the best decision he'd made in ages.

"I'd better get going," Elizabeth said as she stacked her plate in Tish's dishwasher. "Tish, thanks again for breakfast. I'll see you both later . . . although I have no idea when. The schedule says today we'll have an orientation and then read through all three plays, so that could mean anything."

"No problem," Tish responded cheerfully. "Just have a fabulous time. If you get home late, the fridge is full of leftovers, and the microwave is over there." She pointed to a box draped in black velvet on the far end of the kitchen counter. "I like to keep it covered to block the radioactive waves," she explained.

Elizabeth smothered a smile as she scooped her backpack from the floor. "Thanks, Tish." She leaned over the back of Tom's chair to give him a quick kiss on the cheek. "Good luck at your interview. I know you'll do great."

"You too, Liz," Tom returned softly. "Break a leg."

As she headed down the hall to the elevator Elizabeth exhaled deeply. It suddenly occurred to her that she was on her own for the first time since she'd arrived in New York. She felt as if a great weight were being lifted from her . . . or as if the support had been knocked out from under her; she wasn't quite sure which.

When she pushed open the front door of Tish's apartment building, Elizabeth was taken aback by the wave of heat that rose from the pavement to greet her. She could feel the perspiration spring up under the collar of her white oxford shirt. Although it was still early in the summer, the air felt as if it was about ninety degrees. *Must be the greenhouse effect,* Elizabeth figured, recalling what she'd learned about big cities in her environmental science class. *I've never experienced humidity like this!*

As she turned the corner onto Broadway and headed downtown, Elizabeth felt as if she were sleepwalking through a dream world. Brightly colored bodegas, boutiques, and bagel shops lined both sides of the street; lively salsa music spilled out their doors onto the sidewalk. The sidewalks were teeming with people: funky college students in cutoffs, parents pushing strollers, and professionals looking miserable and wilted in their dark business suits. Across the street a cluster of adolescents in bathing suits ran shrieking in circles around an open fire hydrant.

*There's so much going on here, so many different kinds of people,* Elizabeth marveled as she drank in the scene. *It feels like anything could happen . . . like I could turn into someone else if I wanted to.*

In a way, Elizabeth admitted to herself, she felt as if she already *had* turned into someone else since arriving in New York. It was unsettling enough to think that she was on her way to the theater district to direct and produce her own play—something she'd never even dreamed of achieving. But the fact that last night she'd almost convinced herself she was ready for *sex* . . . well, that was enough to make

115

her think she should hail a cab and head straight for Bellevue.

*What's happening to me?* Elizabeth asked herself. Somehow, in this totally different world, she felt completely unconnected to her normal life. The SVU campus, her parents' house on Calico Drive— everything seemed a million miles away. *Maybe for once in my life I should just relax and do what comes naturally without worrying about the consequences.*

*I wish Jess were here,* Elizabeth thought suddenly with the twinge of emptiness she often felt when her twin was far away. *It would be so nice to talk to her right now—she'd know exactly how to put things in perspective.* It wasn't just that her younger sister, once a married woman, was more experienced with men than she was. Jessica just had a lust for life, a thirst for excitement unparalleled in anyone Elizabeth knew. Even though she worried about her impulsive, adventurous sister, Elizabeth also admired her courage. Sometimes she wished she could be more like Jessica in that way: afraid of nothing and always up for a challenge.

"We have to run through *what?*" Jessica squealed, quickly clapping her hand over her mouth. She hadn't meant to think out loud, but Pruitt's description of the obstacle course had caught her by surprise.

"You heard me—through the *swamp!*" Pruitt bellowed. A hint of a smile twitched at her thin lips. "But don't worry, princess—the muck only comes up to your chest or so."

116

*Muck? Up to my chest?* Jessica's stomach lurched. Although the rain had finally died down, the swamp that bordered the compound was still swollen with muddy water—and probably crawling with who knew what kind of disgusting creatures.

"Oh, and by the way, princess—interrupt me one more time, and you're looking at KP duty for the rest of the month," Pruitt continued, still smirking. "Now, once you've waded across the swamp, you'll find a canoe hidden somewhere on the opposite bank. Then you and your partner will paddle that canoe across the *next* stretch of swamp to the road. Find a truck there and drive it back to the starting point. The first team to complete the course will receive fifty points, the second team will collect thirty, and the third ten. It's that simple."

*Simple? As if!* Jessica was beginning to wonder if it was too late to back out of this whole mess. As she fidgeted in discomfort a small object fell out of the narrow side pocket of her pant leg—her travel-size tube of sunscreen. *Uh-oh*, she thought as Pruitt's eagle eyes zeroed in on the tiny white plastic tube.

"Well, what have we here?" Sergeant Pruitt purred, sounding almost happy as she sidled over across the row of recruits. "More . . . *beauty* products, princess?" She spat the word *beauty* as if it were something horribly distasteful to her—which, Jessica noted as she eyed Pruitt's leathery crow's-feet, might well have been the case.

As Pruitt stooped to pick up the tube of sunscreen Jessica fought to keep from trembling. She could feel the other recruits looking sideways at her. The compound was deadly quiet except for the faint sound of rain dripping off the mess hall roof behind them.

"SPF thirty, huh?" Pruitt read off the back of the tube. "I hate to break it to you, toots, but this isn't California, and you're not here to get a tan. I don't see the sun exactly beating down on us, do you?"

"But overcast skies are no protection from harmful UV rays!" Jessica protested, reciting an absolute beauty commandment.

"Oooh, listen to her," Pruitt mocked. Her voice turned stern and menacing. "I'm only going to say this one more time. This is *not* the noon tea at your sorority. This is the next best thing to boot camp. And if you don't get your act together and start paying attention to what's *important*, you're going to be alligator bait!"

"Well, at least I won't get alligator *skin!*" Jessica cried hotly. As soon as the words were out of her mouth a low murmur of laughter ran through the row of recruits. Jessica felt two bright patches of red flame up on her cheeks.

Pruitt set her jaw in a grim line. "I've heard just about enough out of you," she growled. "I will now be assigning partners. There better be no further disruptions from Miss Congeniality!"

Pruitt started barking out names, and the line of recruits began to split apart into pairs. Jessica hoped desperately that she would be paired with Harlan, but he was assigned to a tall, good-looking African American guy.

"Jessica Wakefield and Sunshine Harris!" Pruitt

called. As she stepped forward Jessica found herself face-to-face with her bunk mate: the cigar-smoking redhead.

*Sunshine? She looks about as sunny as the underside of a rock,* Jessica thought as she ventured a timid smile. Judging from Sunshine's expression, she was none too thrilled to be partners with the "princess." Jessica quashed her unreturned smile and swallowed hard.

When all the recruits had been assembled into pairs, Pruitt clapped. "All right, people. Why don't we get a real *pro* to show us how it's done. Will Her Royal Highness, Private Wakefield, accept the honor of being the first one into the swamp?"

Jessica hesitated. Then she saw the glint of challenge in Pruitt's eyes. Taking a deep breath, Jessica squared her shoulders and stepped forward. *I can't let that dried-up bag of bones show me up,* she told herself.

Encouraged by the annoyed look on Pruitt's face, Jessica marched forward into the swamp. The mud was cold, wet, and slimy; the second she was in past her boots, she felt as if it had soaked through to the soles of her feet. *This isn't so bad,* she told herself unconvincingly. *It's just like the mud bath at that spa I went to with Lila!*

By the time she was ten feet out into the swamp, she was mired in muddy water up to her waist. Jessica slowly let out her breath, her squeamishness at the skin-crawling sensation balanced by her triumphant sense of pride at having met Pruitt's challenge. *I'm going to make it!* she cheered mentally.

Just then Jessica had the distinct sensation that

she was not alone in the water. Something was slithering past her leg!

All at once every inch of her body tensed up. Jessica bit down on the inside of her cheek to keep from shrieking. Her eyes searched the water frantically for signs of movement, but the swamp was clouded over with mud.

Jessica forced herself to keep slugging across the swamp. *Whatever horrible, slimy thing is sharing my space,* she told herself grimly, *it couldn't possibly be more terrifying than Sergeant Pruneface.*

As soon as Elizabeth stepped off the air-conditioned train car and into the sweltering underground subway station, she felt perspiration bead up on her forehead. *I'd better start carrying around bottled water, or one of these days I'll pass out,* she told herself as she waded through the palpable heat of the rancid-smelling station.

When Elizabeth had climbed the seemingly endless stairs to street level, she had to pause for breath—and to take stock of the surreal, larger-than-life cityscape that loomed around her. She was standing smack in the middle of Times Square, a narrow yet impossibly built-up fork in the road swarming with crowds. Everywhere she looked, the air was filled with enormous billboards and neon signs large enough to be read clearly from the vast skyscrapers that towered over them.

When she turned onto West Forty-fourth Street, Elizabeth was relieved and delighted to see the huge billboards give way to charming, human-size theater buildings with ornate cornices carved into gargoyles or classical-style nymph figures. Elizabeth slowed her pace to get a closer look at the large posters framed on the theater walls. She couldn't help wondering dreamily what the poster for *her* play would look like.

After walking only a couple of blocks Elizabeth found the Maxwell Theater, home of the Miller Huttleby Foundation plays. It was a small theater covered in chipping white paint with an ancient-looking marquee lined by round white lights. Elizabeth stood still on the sidewalk, absorbing the aura of history emanating from the quaint building.

"Pretty cool, huh?"

Elizabeth turned to see a handsome young man holding a rolled-up stack of paper under his arm. He had delicate features but a strong jawline, and his grin revealed a dimple in his chin. His curly black hair was slicked back with pomade. He was only a few inches taller than Elizabeth but obviously in great shape: the rolled-up sleeves of his white V-neck T-shirt revealed muscular biceps.

For a moment Elizabeth was speechless, unable to comprehend why such a hip and strikingly handsome New Yorker would be stopping to talk to her. He definitely looked familiar—but where could she possibly know him from?

"I said, this theater is pretty cool," the young man repeated. "You know, John Barrymore appeared here back in the day."

"Really?" Elizabeth exclaimed, startled out of

her shyness. "You know, I was just thinking that this place *exudes* nostalgia."

He nodded wisely. "You must be very intuitive. Actors usually are. Are you trying out for this play?" He unrolled the sheaf of paper under his arm and extended it to Elizabeth. The top sheet read *The Eternal Vortex: A Play in One Act,* by Claire Sterling. "Or are you reading for something else? I hear there are three different productions being mounted here."

"Uh, actually," Elizabeth answered with a nervous laugh, "I'm one of the playwrights. Not of the script you're holding, though. Mine is called *Two Sides to Every Story.*"

"Ah, a writer! I'm impressed." His dark eyes twinkled. "Having your play produced off-Broadway is quite an accomplishment for someone so young."

"Well, it's just a student production," Elizabeth hastened to explain. "See, every year this foundation puts on three one-act plays by students. . . ." She trailed off, suddenly struck by just *how* familiar the young man looked. *Maybe someone Jess knows?* she guessed, for some reason getting a foggy picture of him with her sister.

"Student or not, there's quite a buzz about these plays," he insisted. "My agent was all over me about reading for this part. Speaking of which, I'm running a little late. Shall we?" He gestured toward the theater entrance.

"Sure." Elizabeth followed him into the theater,

still racking her brain to figure out if she actually knew the guy or if he just had a familiar kind of face.

The lobby of the Maxwell had the same kind of dilapidated elegance as the exterior of the building. An enormous chandelier that looked as if it hadn't been cleaned in decades hung from the ceiling; the red carpet might once have been plush but was now threadbare.

"The place hasn't been restored in a while," the young man said, echoing Elizabeth's thoughts. "Unlike some of the historical theaters, it doesn't get much funding."

"Why not?" Elizabeth asked. "It's an incredible space."

"No doubt," he agreed. "But theater people are notoriously superstitious. And as legend would have it, there's a curse on this place—supposedly back in the forties a jealous understudy jinxed the leading lady, and ever since then the Maxwell's had a bad vibe. At least that's the excuse whenever a production here flops."

"What a romantic story!" Elizabeth breathed. "How do you know so much about this place?"

The young man shrugged. "I guess I'm just a nerd when it comes to acting lore. Maybe I subconsciously believe one of the random details I dig up is going to make me just as good an actor as one of those legendary guys. Fat chance, right?"

Elizabeth laughed. "You know, if you're going to make it as an actor, you'd better learn to be a little more full of yourself."

The young man grinned. "Thanks. I'll make a

note of that. It was nice meeting you, but I've got to run."

Elizabeth lingered in the lobby for a minute, savoring the good feeling she got from the Maxwell, curse and all. To her the theater was much more appealing than if it had been new and flashy like everything else in Times Square. There was a certain charm to a place with a past—especially a past involving the ghosts of legendary theater figures. Elizabeth felt a thrill of anticipation run down her spine as she realized that she was going to become a part—however small—of the Maxwell's history.

Whistling an aimless but cheerful little melody, Tom straightened his tie and ran a hand through his hair. He glanced behind him in the elevator's round security mirror to make sure he didn't look too wilted from his subway ride and his walk in the sweltering heat. But as far as he could tell, he was presentable.

The elevator doors opened, and Tom peered out onto the twenty-eighth floor. Dozens of cardboard boxes lined one wall of the long corridor. *Is this the right place?* Tom wondered, nervously tugging his tie as he stepped tentatively into the hallway. *It looks more like a storage facility than a production office!*

A door at the end of the corridor opened, and a harried-looking guy emerged, carrying a box.

"Excuse me," Tom called out. "Is this Sandy Cove Productions?"

The guy looked up and let out a sarcastic little

snort. "Yeah. Yeah, for whatever it's worth, this is Sandy Cove."

Puzzled, Tom followed him through the door to the production office—and almost tripped over a metal filing cabinet that was resting on a hand truck propped against the wall. Startled, he glanced around and saw that papers, file folders, videotapes, and half-packed boxes were strewn across the desks and floor. Everywhere Tom looked, young men and women were busily throwing office equipment into boxes, rooting through desk drawers, or prying loose items that were bolted to the floor or walls. *Looks like the place is being looted!* Tom thought in bewilderment. *Maybe they're expanding to a different office.*

Tom approached a woman who was crouching on the floor and unscrewing cables from the back of her computer "Excuse me—sorry to bother you, but can you tell me where I can find Ira Rosenzweig? I have an interview with him at noon."

Without looking up, the woman pointed toward a side corridor. Tom thanked her and hurried away. After making a series of twists and turns down the dim, narrow hall, Tom found the office. A brass nameplate swung on the door by one screw and read I. Rosenzweig, Executive Producer.

Tom peered in through the open door. Inside, a thirtyish dark-haired man was bent over a box on the floor, rifling through its contents. Tom hovered uncertainly for a second, cleared his throat, and rapped on the door frame.

The man in the office looked up in surprise. "Yes?" he snapped, straightening up. "Can I help you?"

"Uh—yes—that is—I hope—" Flustered, Tom extended his arm. "Mr. Rosenzweig? Tom Watts. I'm your twelve o'clock?"

"My tw—" Mr. Rosenzweig sighed and pressed his palms to his brow as if he were trying to keep his head from exploding. "Well, Mr. Watts, thanks for your time, but I'm afraid we won't be needing your services. Sandy Cove was just purchased by the Unicom Conglomerate, and they're firing the entire production staff. Including the people we haven't hired yet."

Tom felt as if the wind had been knocked out of him. His professional demeanor dissolving, he leaned against the door frame to keep his knees from buckling.

"But—but—what am I going to *do?*" he stammered, hearing the note of panic in his own voice.

A bitter laugh escaped Mr. Rosenzweig's lips as he bent over the cardboard box again. "Funny—after giving this place five years of my life, I was just wondering the same thing myself." He glared up at Tom. "I *can* give you *one* piece of advice, though."

"What's that?" Tom asked eagerly.

"Don't let the door hit your butt on your way out."

# Chapter Ten

"Land ho!" Sunshine shouted triumphantly. She raised her arms over her head and put on a burst of speed to trudge through the last few feet of swamp.

*What did she just call me?* Jessica wondered, narrowing her eyes suspiciously as she followed her partner out of the bog. All the way across the swamp Sunshine had made sarcastic remarks whenever Jessica squealed, stumbled, or complained, but she hadn't yet resorted to outright name-calling.

"OK, Wakefield, do you see the canoe anywhere?" Sunshine stood on the bank of the swamp, shielding her eyes with her forearm. Leafy ferns and lush vegetation made it impossible to see more than a couple of yards in any direction. "It's gotta be around here somewhere."

"No," Jessica panted as she scrambled onto the slippery bank. Pausing to catch her breath, she scanned the mud-sodden landscape. Through a clearing in the trees she could see another stretch of swamp. "What about heading that way?" she suggested, pointing.

"That's as good a plan as any," Sunshine conceded.

The two women slogged across the muddy stretch of land, digging in their heels where it sloped steeply down toward the next stretch of swamp. When they reached the edge, Jessica saw a mass of crisscrossed fern boughs floating suspiciously in the water. "You think that's the canoe?" she asked excitedly, turning to Sunshine.

The redhead nodded curtly. "Is the Pope Catholic? Just help me get those ferns off it."

The canoe bobbed up and down as Jessica and Sunshine cleared the boughs off its surface. When it was completely uncovered, Sunshine grabbed the side of the boat with her hands and swung her leg over it. The canoe teetered precariously.

"You're going to tip it over," Jessica declared, remembering what she'd learned as a summer camp counselor in high school. "Here, let me help." She waded into the swamp and stood behind the canoe, bracing it with her hands on both sides. She looked up at Sunshine expectantly.

Sunshine opened her mouth as if she was about to object, then set her jaw tightly and got into the canoe.

Jessica picked up one of the oars and stuck it upright into the muddy bottom of the swamp. Then, moving very slowly and using the oar to support her weight, she managed to climb into the canoe without tipping it over. *Go, girl!* Jessica cheered as she gradually let out her breath.

Sunshine reached for her oar and wordlessly began to paddle. Jessica did the same, feeling the slightest bit disappointed that her partner refused to acknowledge her genius. *What do I have to do to live down this dumb-blonde stereotype?* she wondered bitterly as they rowed in silence.

"Hey!" Sunshine suddenly hissed. "Do you see that?"

"See what?" Jessica blinked. They were yards from shore now; gray swamp water stretched in every direction. "I don't see anything."

Sunshine pointed a trembling finger at the edge of the canoe. *"That,"* she whispered in a quivering voice.

Jessica followed the line of Sunshine's finger to the rim of the canoe and felt her blood run cold. Along the side of the boat something was *slithering* . . . a gleaming green snake, about as big around as Jessica's wrist and who knew *how* long. For a second Jessica couldn't find its head. Then she saw it—headed straight for her end of the boat.

"We have to *do* something!" Sunshine urged, staring at the slimy reptile as if it had hypnotized her. "I—I *hate* snakes!"

As she spoke, the snake lifted its diamond-shaped head and flitted out its tongue as if it were licking its chops.

Jessica hesitated only a second. "Here, hold this!" she commanded, handing over her oar. She reached into the cargo pocket on her pant leg and pulled out her pink flowered plastic makeup bag.

Sunshine's jaw dropped. "Have you gone off the deep end?" she cried. "What are you going to do—give the snake a makeover?"

Jessica didn't respond—there wasn't time. The snake was inches from her arm. Finally she located her travel-size can of hair spray and the matches she used to soften her eyeliner. With shaking hands she struck a match.

*Thank goodness I didn't let Liz the Tree Hugger force me to go nonaerosol,* Jessica thought as she held up the lit match in front of the snake and pressed the nozzle on her hair spray.

With a loud *foomp* a stream of blue flame shot out into the air. Through the fumes Jessica saw the snake disappear under the dark surface of the swamp.

She looked up to see Sunshine frozen stock-still, her mouth gaping. Her face was ashen; even her freckles seemed drained of color. Jessica couldn't keep a smug smile from creeping across her face.

"Sorry, what were you saying?" she asked Sunshine sweetly, dropping the can of hair spray back into her bag. "Oh, of course—makeovers. You're right, I have been known to do them on occasion. I can give you one when we get back to the barracks if you'd like."

Sunshine glared at Jessica, but her clenched mouth relaxed into a grudging grin. Jessica beamed. *Being a princess is kind of cool sometimes,* she decided.

*I wish I knew someone here,* Elizabeth thought as two tall, stick-thin girls in black dresses threw back

130

their heads in shared laughter. As much as she loved the building itself, Elizabeth felt out of place at the Maxwell. There were dozens of other young people milling around the lobby, chatting or running lines in groups of two and three. Almost without exception they were dressed in the same funky-yet-sophisticated outfits Elizabeth had seen in the West Village. She looked down at her own white oxford and khakis and felt like what Jessica would have called an "antifashion victim."

Just then Elizabeth felt a tap on her shoulder. "Excuse me, but are you Elizabeth Wakefield?"

Elizabeth turned to see a tall, lanky man who looked to be in his midthirties giving her a friendly smile. His unruly mop of shoulder-length brown hair brushed the shoulders of his black tuxedo shirt. Below the hems of his black jeans—she noticed with a mild start—he was barefoot.

"Uh, yes," Elizabeth said slowly. "I'm sorry, but have we met?"

The man threw back his head and laughed a loud, theatrical laugh. "No, no, no, darling. I'm Ted Kelly, head producer and dramaturge for the Miller Huttleby Foundation. I just wanted to run out and nab you for a little creative meeting–slash–orientation meeting backstage with me and the other playwrights."

"Sure, but how did you know—"

He let out another over-the-top laugh. "Lucky guess, darling. Your file said you were from California, and, well, you look like you've seen a lot more sun than anyone else."

Ted led Elizabeth to a large dressing room backstage. A young man and woman about Elizabeth's age sat on a worn-out couch. The man had a goatee and was wearing wire-rimmed glasses, a black turtleneck, and jeans. His brown hair was tied back in a ponytail, but in front his hairline was prematurely receding.

The young woman was unlike anyone Elizabeth had *ever* seen. She was dressed all in black with a large spiked leather collar around her neck. Her eyes and lips were heavily lined in black, and her mouth was painted a deep bloodred. Her dyed-black hair was pulled back off her face, and either she was wearing several coats of ultrapale white foundation makeup or she had literally spent the last ten years of her life underground. *How does she walk around in this heat without all that stuff dripping off her face?* Elizabeth wondered.

"Elizabeth Wakefield, meet Gerald van Houten and Claire Sterling," Ted announced.

For professionalism's sake, Elizabeth smiled brightly at her new colleagues. "Hi, Gerald, Claire. It's nice to meet you. I'm looking forward to working with you both."

The room was silent. Gerald wrinkled his nose and inclined his head as if he peevishly thought Elizabeth was a waste of his time. Claire rolled her eyes and puffed out her cheeks, looking bored and too full of contempt to acknowledge Elizabeth's presence.

"OK, great!" Ted clapped and looked from Elizabeth to Gerald to Claire. "Now that we're all acquainted, why don't we get comfortable." He headed for one of two overstuffed chairs and indicated for Elizabeth to take the other. "I'll just go over a few details, and then we'll get started with a read through."

Elizabeth perched uncomfortably on the armchair, annoyed by how Gerald and Claire were too "cool" to be polite to her. She was confident that her play was as good as either of theirs—why couldn't they show her a little respect?

"So after the auditions we'll work together to make final casting decisions," Ted explained. "Then we'll have a few sessions with set designers and work out some preliminary blocking."

Claire was looking at the ceiling. Gerald was looking at his nails. Elizabeth settled back in her chair, trying to imagine how she'd describe them to Tom later. Claire's fashion sense would be the first thing she mentioned, of course. She could just picture Tom's face as he laughed in disbelief, his eyes crinkling up adorably. He'd sweep her into his arms, still laughing, and then . . .

*And then what?* Elizabeth wondered, an involuntary shudder running through her as she flashed back to the night before. Would she and Tom generate that kind of heat again tonight? And if they did, would she be able to maintain her self-control?

"So!" Ted brought his hands together in another thundering clap. "Unless anyone has any questions, let's get started with the read through."

*I've got to get a grip,* Elizabeth thought, disconcerted, as Ted began passing out copies of the scripts. *No matter how intense things get with Tom,*

*I'm here to put on a play. I have to stay focused!*

"One hot dog with mustard, please."

The vendor squinted at Tom as he handed the hot dog across the cart. "Didn't I see you here about an hour ago?"

Tom nodded sheepishly as he handed over his money. "I've, uh, I've been sightseeing. I must've walked in a circle." As he walked away he cringed at his own fib.

*Nice, Watts—you've stooped to lying to random members of the service industry,* he berated himself as he took a bite of his hot dog. But he couldn't stand the thought of telling anyone, even a stranger, the truth: that he'd just been walking around aimlessly, feeling sorry for himself.

In the thick heat of crowded midtown Manhattan, Tom felt as if he were moving in slow motion. His suit was sticking to his body, and strands of damp hair clung to his forehead; he felt as if he might melt into the sidewalk at any minute. Despite all his confidence this morning he was wandering the city with no job, no prospects, no connections, and a rapidly dwindling bank account that wasn't going to cushion him much longer—especially if he wanted to impress his girlfriend. His head was hanging so low that the only sights he'd seen were his feet on the pavement.

*Get a grip,* he ordered himself, stopping short on a corner. *You're not moving from this spot until you figure out where you're headed.* Somewhere there had to be a decent summer job where a talented

134

young man could earn some experience.

An image of himself in L.A., sitting with his feet up on the intern desk, flashed through his mind, and for a second Tom thought he might cry.

He shook his head to clear the mental picture. *I can't just spend the summer kicking myself,* he decided. *That'd be laying a huge guilt trip on Liz. I'm here for her, and I've got to make the best of this summer.*

Tom gazed up at the huge office buildings that loomed all around him. On this one block alone there were probably five buildings with fifty stories each. Somewhere, behind one of those millions of windows, there just had to be a vacant office with his name on it. The only question was how he was going to find it.

For what seemed like ages Tom stood on the sidewalk, watching the cars and buses speed by . . . watching the world pass him by, it felt like. Then the light turned red, and the traffic slowed. An ad on the side of a city bus caught Tom's eye. Channel 11 Local News at 10, it read. New York City in Your Backyard!

Tom squared his shoulders and started walking up the street at a brisk pace, fueled by anticipation. What had he been thinking, moping around aimlessly in the middle of the Big Apple? If he could make it here, he could make it anywhere, right?

*So what if I have no connections?* Tom asked himself. *If I show some spirit,* someone *will take a chance on me, right?*

He spotted a policeman at the next corner. "Excuse me, Officer," Tom called out as he approached, flashing his brightest job-interview smile to get himself into the groove. "Can you direct me to the nearest network building?"

Jessica pulled the wooden oar toward her with all her might, feeling as if every inch of flesh on the palms of her hands were filled with splinters. But no matter how hard she strained, she couldn't match the effortless strokes of Sunshine's muscular arms. Jessica didn't think it was possible for a canoe to drag its behind, but that was exactly what this one seemed to be doing.

"Hey, Wakefield," Sunshine spoke up suddenly. "You a good driver?"

Jessica blinked, startled. "Yeah," she panted between oar strokes. "Why?"

"Well, no offense, but you look like you're about to turn purple," Sunshine observed. "So if you want to take it easy for a while, I don't mind picking up the slack—then when we get to shore, you can drive the truck and *I* can rest."

"Oh, but—" Jessica hesitated. Was Sunshine testing her, trying to see how easily she would give up? "No, really, I'm fine." With a little grunt she gave the oars an extra harsh tug for emphasis.

"Honestly—don't exhaust yourself now, or you'll be ready to drop by the end of the course," Sunshine pointed out. "That's why we work in pairs—so we can cover for our partners if we have to. It's not a big deal." She flashed Jessica a crooked smile.

"Well . . . if you say so. Thanks." Slowly Jessica relaxed her grip on the oars, unclenching her stiff, red fingers. She was surprised and slightly embarrassed to notice that although she was now paddling with only half the effort, the canoe hardly seemed to have slowed down at all. Sunshine, unlike Jessica, had obviously given *her* copy of *Upper Body of Steel* a real workout.

"No problem," Sunshine replied casually. "But you *better* be a good driver."

"I'm a *great* driver," Jessica declared. "I grew up near L.A., remember? I was practically *raised* on the freeway."

The two women exchanged a grin, and Jessica couldn't help feeling a teensy bit gratified. *Sunshine still doesn't exactly live up to her name in the personality department,* Jessica decided. *But at least now she's only . . . partly cloudy.* Hopefully the rest of her barrack mates would come around too—and soon.

"Alone, alone, alone," Gerald intoned in a vibrato voice as he sucked in his cheeks. His pale, goateed face looked wan and gaunt above his black turtleneck. "We are all infected with the loneliness for which there is no cure. Infected . . . afflicted . . . *alone.*"

Elizabeth stifled a yawn. It was remotely possible that Gerald was a genius whose profound work was beyond her understanding. But it struck her as much more likely that he was a pretentious bore whose play, *Leviathan Inferno,* rambled and made no sense. His shrill falsetto seemed to have been droning unintelligible dialogue for hours, and so far the only advancement in the plot was that an old man had taken a bite of an apple.

"We are all sick! Alone! No cure!" Gerald concluded in a stage whisper. Switching to his normal voice, he continued, "The jester exits stage right, leaving the old man alone onstage. The old man drops the apple and crumples to the floor."

*At least this is better than* Claire's *play,* Elizabeth conceded, hiding a wry grimace behind her script as she turned the page. *Her* The Eternal Vortex *makes this sound like* Death of a Salesman. *If nothing else, it was aptly titled.* After following along with the script for an hour as Claire mumbled her way through endless free-association monologues about postmodern malaise, existential angst, and the anger in her womb, Elizabeth would have been impressed by a dramatic reading of a passage from the white pages.

Glancing around, she suddenly realized that the room was silent, and Gerald was slumped on the couch like a boxer who'd just gone ten rounds. *That's it? The play is over?* Elizabeth thought in disbelief. *Nothing happened! It made no sense!*

Claire's face was expressionless as ever. *But Ted actually seems* . . . moved? *By that pretentious nonsense?* Elizabeth wondered, unable to understand how the producer could be nodding as seriously as he was. He almost appeared to be getting slightly misty-eyed.

"That was *amazing,* Gerald," Ted said in a voice that sounded far too reverent to be sincere. "I'm surprised that someone your age has such a wise perspective on mortality." He clapped briskly and

138

replaced his clouded expression with a broad smile. "OK, so that leaves Elizabeth. Elizabeth, are you ready to begin?" Ted turned to fix her with the same earnest look he'd just been training on Gerald. "We're all very eager to hear your work."

*Yeah, right,* Elizabeth thought, glancing over at Gerald's self-satisfied half smile and Claire's haughty mask of utter disdain. *They look like they're practically jumping out of their seats.* Not that she cared whether or not her so-called colleagues were interested in her work. Now that she'd heard them read through their absurd plays and heard Ted's obviously excessive praise, Elizabeth wasn't the least bit nervous about reading through her own script.

"Sure, I'm ready," Elizabeth affirmed, returning Ted's smile as brightly and confidently as she could. *Ted is going to love it,* she assured herself as she picked up her script. Obviously a witty romantic comedy set in a newsroom provided more professional and polished entertainment than the bizarre ravings of two depressed misfits.

"'Two Sides to Every Story,'" Elizabeth read aloud. "'Scene I. The WBIQ newsroom, late at night. Gavin is hunched over his desk, typing furiously. Phoebe enters, carrying an armful of tapes.'

"'Phoebe: Any new leads?'" she continued, reading the first line of dialogue in what she hoped was a far more natural-sounding voice than Gerald or Claire had used. "'Gavin: Nope. The athletics department covered its tracks pretty well. But I'm sure we'll dig up some dirt pretty soon.'"

Just then Gerald cleared his throat. Momentarily

startled, Elizabeth looked up in time to see him and Claire glance briefly at each other and then look away. Gerald suddenly lifted up his script to cover his face while Claire rolled her eyes toward the ceiling.

*Whatever,* Elizabeth thought as she resumed reading her script. She couldn't have cared less what those two self-important snobs thought of her play. What was important was that *Ted* knew her work was good. *He* was the professional.

As she flipped the first page of her script Elizabeth stole a peek at Ted's face—and almost lost her place. For a second it looked as if *he* was smirking too.

Tom almost gasped when the elevator doors opened onto a scene that seemed more suited to a luxury spa than an office building. The fiftieth-floor lobby of WNYK Studios was as large as Tish's whole apartment and had gleaming, polished gray slate walls. The wall behind the huge circular reception desk was made up entirely of glowing TV screens. By the time he reached the reception desk, Tom was shaking in his dress shoes.

*What made me think I could just waltz in here and ask for a job?* he berated himself. *I've been turned away everywhere else.*

Tom was rapidly discovering that New York City wasn't as eager to take a chance on young talent as he'd thought. He'd been circling the West Thirties for the better part of two hours, and this was only the fourth time he'd made it as far as the reception area. The security guards usually sent him on his way as soon as he admitted he didn't have an appointment or even a lead.

*The fact that my suit is practically stuck to my body probably doesn't improve my chances,* Tom thought ruefully. *I've sweated off at least five pounds just by walking up and down Fifth Avenue.*

The receptionist, an African American woman dressed in a crisp business suit with an impossibly starched collar, eyed Tom with barely veiled disdain. "May I *help* you?" she asked almost accusingly.

"Hi, I'm Tom Watts," Tom said, summoning up every shred of confidence he had left. He was about to extend his hand but quickly withdrew it; his palm was clammy with sweat. "I'm a student at Sweet Valley University out in California and the news director for its TV station, WSVU. I'm in town for the summer, and I was hoping to speak to someone about any job openings you might have."

The receptionist pursed her lips for a moment, then pointed one perfectly French-manicured finger at Tom. "Actually we *do* have a college-level position open. If you don't mind taking a seat over there, I'll put in a call to the personnel manager." She indicated an elegant black leather sectional couch that ran along one wall.

*Yes!* Tom cheered silently as he perched on the edge of the stiff, uncomfortable couch. *I have an in!*

He wasn't sure exactly what the receptionist had meant by "college level"—but he didn't really care. He'd be grateful for any broadcasting experience he could gain.

"Mr. Watts?"

141

Tom looked up to see a tall, smiling man in a gray suit. "Yes, sir!" he said eagerly, jumping to his feet.

"I'm Pete Barsoum, personnel manager of WNYK."

Tom extended a now reasonably dry hand. "It's a pleasure to meet you, Mr. Barsoum. Thanks for taking the time to see me on such short notice."

"Sure thing, Tom. Why don't we step into my office?"

Mr. Barsoum led Tom into a corner office with a spectacular view of the city and the river. The personnel manager sat down behind a gigantic mahogany desk and gestured for Tom to take a seat opposite him. "So, Tom," he began. "The position we have in mind is a pretty big responsibility. You'll be dealing with everyone at the network. Do you think you can handle that?"

"Absolutely," Tom asserted in his best interview voice. "I view challenges as opportunities. Would you like to see my resume? I've got it right here in my—"

Mr. Barsoum waved him aside. "That won't be necessary. Frankly, we really need someone right away. The last guy quit very abruptly, and we're extremely shorthanded. Could you start tomorrow?"

"I sure could!" Tom straightened up in his seat, trying not to grin too goofily. *That was easier than I thought!* he exulted, imagining what it would be like to work in this glamorous building. Obviously Mr. Barsoum had seen some kind of spark in him. "So what exactly does the job entail? It sounds fascinating."

Mr. Barsoum gave him a funny look. "Didn't the

142

receptionist explain?" When Tom responded with a blank look, the personnel manager went on. "Well, it involves a little prep work and cleanup, but mostly you'll just be serving. We'll need you to come in at eight for the breakfast rush, but you can leave at three as long as the cafeteria is cleaned up."

Tom's mouth dropped open, and for a moment he was speechless. *The cafeteria?* his mind screamed. That's *where my foot in the door got me? A food service job?*

Tom clamped his mouth shut and shook his head. He felt like such an idiot. A minute ago he'd been convinced that he radiated competence. Now he knew *anyone* could have walked in off the street and gotten a job waiting on the network VIPs.

"I'm sorry, Mr. Barsoum," he said, rising to his feet, "but I'm looking for a career in TV journalism, not in food service. Thanks anyway for your time."

# Chapter Eleven

"We made it!" Jessica cheered as she swung her leg over the side of the canoe. The muddy water went halfway up her calf, but she didn't blink an eye; she was so relieved to be out of the swamp that she had genuinely stopped caring about her appearance.

"Not a minute too soon, man," Sunshine panted as they waded through the shallow water to the bank. "I feel like my arms are about to fall off."

"Look, there's the truck." Jessica pointed toward a dirt road, visible through a clearing in the trees. "Let's go!"

"Remember, you're driving," Sunshine grunted as they jogged toward the truck.

Jessica ran around to the driver's side of the truck and climbed in as Sunshine slid in beside her. There was a key already in the ignition, but when she turned it, the engine sputtered and died.

"What's wrong?" Sunshine demanded. "Why isn't the truck starting?"

"I don't know!" Jessica waited, pumped the gas three times with her foot, and turned the key again. The engine made a straining, wheezing noise, then was silent. "It's broken!" she wailed.

Sunshine sighed, opened the passenger-side door, and jumped out of the truck. Jessica popped the hood, opened her own door, and met Sunshine at the front of the truck. Sunshine had lifted up the hood and was staring intently at the engine.

"I can't tell what's wrong," Sunshine declared after a minute. "I mean, I'm no pro mechanic, but I know my way around a carburetor, and this one looks A-OK to me."

"What should we *do?*" Jessica moaned, glancing wildly around in exasperation. The road stretched into the jungle of trees around the swamp as far as Jessica could see. She had no idea how long it would take if they had to get back to the compound on foot.

Suddenly something glinting in the dirt a few feet away caught Jessica's eye. She stooped to get a closer look. "My sunscreen!" she exclaimed in surprise, reaching out to pick up the tube. "But how did this get here? I dropped it, and . . ."

*Pruitt!* Jessica's heart plummeted into her stomach as the implications sank in. *She's been here—and she messed with our truck!* She looked at Sunshine, who whistled slowly and shook her head.

"Girl, Sergeant Pruitt has it *in* for you," Sunshine warned as she slammed the hood shut. "Well, let's hope she just messed with the ignition, not the engine. I'll hot-wire this puppy and see what happens."

Sunshine stuck her head through the driver's-side doorway. Jessica could see her arms grappling with something under the steering wheel. As Sunshine worked Jessica reeled with the sudden awareness of just how vindictive Pruitt could be. Half of her wanted to throw in the towel and go home, but the other half was determined to stay—and to make Pruitt sorry she'd ever scapegoated Jessica Wakefield.

The loud purr of the engine roused Jessica from her thoughts. Sunshine let out a triumphant whoop and climbed all the way into the truck.

"That was totally awesome!" Jessica gushed, climbing into the driver's seat as Sunshine scooted over to make room for her. "You have to show me how to do that sometime."

"Sometime," Sunshine agreed, her jaw set in determination. "For now let's just concentrate on making up lost time. I want to see Pruitt's face when we show up in first place."

"I heard *that*," Jessica agreed as she revved up the engine. "Hang on—I'll get us there as fast as I can."


"'I love you too, Gavin. Now let's get back to work,'" Elizabeth read with feeling. "'Phoebe and Gavin break away from their embrace, sit back down at their desks, and begin typing furiously. Fade to black.'"

Her voice exhausted, she leaned back in her chair and looked up expectantly at the others. *I can't wait to hear what Ted has to say,* she thought proudly.

147

The room was quiet. Unsurprisingly Gerald and Claire were wearing their usual half-blank, half-amused expressions. But Ted's face was pursed into an almost pained look, as if he were at a loss for words.

Elizabeth felt her face grow hot. The silence was excruciating. She knew her play was good, or it wouldn't have earned her the fellowship. So why wasn't anyone complimenting her?

"Thoughts? Anyone?" Ted asked finally.

Gerald opened his mouth, closed it, then opened it again. "It's very . . . *linear,*" he said at last. "I felt that it had a totally unproblematized modernist sensibility."

*"Unproblematized?"* Elizabeth thought in bewilderment. *Why does that* not *sound like a rave review to me?*

Ted nodded thoughtfully. "OK. Interesting. Claire?"

Claire shrugged. "I felt that it was extremely essentialist and rather reductionist as well."

Ted steepled his fingers together and pressed them to his lips, still nodding. "These are all good points. But luckily we do have some time before we open, so let's think about ways of . . . retooling."

Elizabeth felt like her heart had just been ripped in two. She wasn't sure about the exact meaning of the jargon Gerald and Claire were tossing around, but she wasn't so dense as to miss the sentiment behind it—that they thought her play was laughably bad. Elizabeth wouldn't have cared—after hearing *their* work, she didn't hold either Gerald's *or*

148

Claire's opinion in very high regard. But what stung was that Ted seemed to agree with them.

*When he raved about their plays, I was sure he was just being polite,* Elizabeth thought, crestfallen. *But he must have been serious . . . since he can't find one nice thing to say about mine! Was my play really worse than those two?*


"Tom? Tom Watts? Is that you? I don't believe it!"

A massive belly laugh resounded behind Tom, who froze in his tracks. He was sure he knew that booming voice—although in the context of Fifth Avenue, he couldn't quite place it.

Tom turned around to see Dex Chase, a beefy, good-natured guy who had graduated from SVU a year ago, standing on the sidewalk. Tom knew him through several of his old football buddies, who'd been Dex's frat brothers. Dex's expensive-looking blue suit was in much better shape than Tom's, and he was carrying an elegant briefcase.

"Dex," Tom said weakly, feeling embarrassed to be caught looking so disheveled. "What a coincidence. How's it going?"

"Awesome!" Dex boomed. "Pulling down sixty Gs doing financial consulting for Fortune 500 firms. I've got a penthouse on the Upper East Side. Things are really *jelling* for me."

"Wow, Dex. Way to go," Tom said, managing a less than sincere smile. Sure, Dex was an OK guy, but that didn't mean Tom was in the mood to hear his success story.

"But hey, what am I saying?" Dex exclaimed,

punching Tom affectionately on the shoulder. "All that probably sounds like small potatoes to a BMOC like you, right? Football star, TV news anchor, dean's list student . . . So which one of your many projects brings you to New York?"

"Well, uh . . ." Tom hesitated, racking his brain. *I can't exactly admit that I chased after my girlfriend and ended up jobless,* he noted painfully. *How pathetic would that sound?*

"No, no, don't tell me," Dex went on, waving his hands. "You won a grant to make a documentary. Or—let's see—you got a scholarship to a summer program at some grad school. C'mon, I'm sure you won't make me feel *too* inadequate."

Tom wished with all his heart that he hadn't been such an arrogant, attention-craving jerk back when he'd played on the football team. Maybe then he wouldn't have created such an unrealistic reputation for himself. *There's no way I can tell Dex the truth,* Tom thought with a grimace. *If I fessed up, I'd feel ten times as foolish as I already do—and that's saying a* lot.

"Uh, I can't really discuss it right now, Dex," Tom fudged. "The project is sort of under wraps, but I'll be sure to let you know as soon as I can." *Like whenever I actually get a job,* he added silently.

"Sounds intriguing," Dex enthused with another belly laugh. He reached into his breast pocket and pulled out a small leather case. "Give me a call anytime, and we'll go get a beer some night after work," he said, handing Tom a business card. "It was super running into you, Watts, but I'm sure your plate's as full as mine. So we'll get together for that beer, huh?" He clapped Tom on the shoulder and took off.

"Super," Tom echoed hollowly as he clutched the business card in his damp palm. *I've sunk to an all-time low,* he lamented as he tossed Dex's card into a trash can. *"Under wraps"... how lame!*

Suddenly Tom couldn't bear the idea of being rejected anymore. He'd been walking for hours in the heat. He was exhausted and mentally drained—not to mention bedraggled and probably reeking of stale sweat. *There's no way I could land a respectable job in this condition anyway,* Tom conceded bitterly. *I'm going back to Tish's to chill out.*

Jessica slammed on the brakes, and the truck screeched to a halt not ten feet from an ashen-faced Sergeant Pruitt. As she unbuckled her seat belt Jessica saw a grin spread across Sunshine's face.

"You had me worried for a second there," Sunshine admitted. "I didn't think you were going to stop."

Jessica giggled. "Oh, I don't need to run Pruitt over. The look on her face is revenge enough."

*And it sure is sweet,* she added, smiling slyly as she gazed through the windshield at Sergeant Pruitt. *Pruneface looks like she's about to explode. I bet she didn't expect us to make it back at all, much less so soon.*

For a second Jessica thought they had actually

won first place, but then she saw another truck parked in the dirt at the edge of the compound. As she stepped out of the truck Jessica saw Harlan and his partner standing beside the vehicle. *Well, if we had to come in second, at least it's to someone I like,* Jessica mused.

"Hey, congratulations!" Jessica called out to Harlan as she ran across the mud toward him. When he lifted his arm, she high-fived him.

"You're not too shabby yourself," Harlan pointed out with a devilish wink. "There's no shame in coming in second to *me.*"

Jessica fought the urge to roll her eyes. Harlan definitely *didn't* have a low self-esteem problem. "Well, thanks, I think. I feel like I did OK for my first day."

Harlan chuckled and tweaked the brim of her cap. "I'm just giving you a hard time, kid. You were incredible! I'm a big guy, and *I* had a tough time dragging an oar through that mud." His eyes raked appreciatively up and down her uniform. "I don't know where you're hiding all those muscles—everything looks perfectly proportioned to me."

Jessica was about to flip her hair flirtatiously over her shoulder when she remembered that the few strands hanging loose from her cap were encrusted in mud. She settled for flashing Harlan a demure smile. "Well, my partner *did* help a *little,*" she allowed.

"Wakefield!" a voice behind her bellowed.

Jessica whirled around to see Sergeant Pruitt headed straight toward them, her face as purple as an eggplant and her eyes blazing with anger. *Uh-oh,* Jessica thought, her heart sinking. *I'm really in for it this time.* Out of the corner of her eye she could see Harlan backing slowly away from her, as if she were contagious.

*"Wakefield!"* Pruitt barked at the top of her lungs. "Do I have to remind you that this is not a sorority social? I don't care if you came in second— that is no excuse for fraternizing! Report for KP duty at the mess hall in one hour, *princess!"*

Jessica was about to protest, but she swallowed her words instantly. *It's so totally unjust!* Jessica thought, enraged. *It's just like Sunshine said— Pruitt has it in for me.* She glanced around to look for her partner, hoping for some support.

Just then Jessica spotted Sunshine, standing beside a truck that had just pulled up—into third place—a few yards away. She was talking to someone in the truck and lighting a cigar at the same time. As Sunshine took her first puff the driver's-side door opened, and Sunshine's friends—the bleached-blond African American and the pretty, long-haired Filipina—climbed out of the truck. The three women huddled in a circle, whispering. As Jessica stood watching, each woman in turn lifted her face and darted a glance in Jessica's direction, then burst into laughter.

*They're* laughing *at me,* Jessica realized, her heart sinking like a stone. *Sunshine doesn't respect me at all!* Maybe her partner had only been civil to her so they'd get through the obstacle course. *Or maybe she wanted me to open up to her so the Three*

*Musketeers could make fun of me later,* she added. Either way Jessica felt her confidence evaporating like a cloud of cheap styling mist.

"Harris! Vernon! Polanco!" Pruitt barked. "Over here! On the double!"

Jessica felt almost gratified as Sunshine and her pals exchanged looks, slowly filed toward Pruitt, and assembled before her in a line. *At least somebody else is getting called out on the carpet for once,* she thought happily.

"Harris, you've obviously been spending too much time around the princess," Pruitt accused, stepping up to Sunshine and waving a bony finger at her impassive freckled face. "Maybe it slipped your mind that I have a strict policy against fraternization. KP duty should refresh all your memories. Be at the mess hall in an hour!"

Jessica gulped as she watched the three women exchange outraged looks. *If they hated me before,* she thought, her stomach churning with dread, *what now? Pruitt's punishment could be nothing compared to what those three can dish out when she's not around!*

*Very narrative driven,* Elizabeth read. *The characters conform to hegemonically structured subject positions—was this a deliberate choice?*

"Of course it wasn't a deliberate choice, Ted!" she muttered aloud. "I have no idea what you're talking about!" Even though the subway car was full of people, Elizabeth didn't care if she was heard. Besides, the noise of the train rumbling

154

through the tunnel drowned everything out anyway.

She turned over another page of her play, squinting to read the scribbled notes that practically covered the sheet. *How am I going to make all these changes if I have no idea what they mean?* Elizabeth wondered despairingly. She could just hear Gerald and Claire snickering as she asked Ted to explain what was so bad about a play having a narrative.

The D train screeched to a halt, and the doors opened. Elizabeth didn't look up from her script as people streamed on and off the train around her. She couldn't tear her eyes from the maze of red ink scratches that covered her neat lines of type. *Too restrained . . . This doesn't feel honest. . . . Holding back emotion . . . I have trouble trusting these characters. . . .* Each of Ted's margin notes was like a slap in her face.

Elizabeth exhaled deeply as the train jerked to a start again. She'd poured a lot of herself and her feelings into her play, and a good deal of it was taken directly from her experiences with Tom. Hearing Ted's criticisms now, when she was so confused about her relationship, cut through her like a knife. It was as if he was saying *her* emotions were repressed and dishonest.

*Am I holding back emotion?* Elizabeth wondered. *Does our relationship have the same problems the play has?*

*Maybe I'm just reading too much into these notes,* Elizabeth conceded, looking up from the script as her eyes blurred with unshed tears. *Maybe all Ted's saying is that my play stinks.*

While she struggled to decipher another scrawl, the train made another stop. Elizabeth barely registered it as the businessman next to her got up and an Indian woman in a sari sat down in his place. *This ride is taking forever,* she thought miserably as the train started up again. *I just want to get back to Tish's so I can curl up in a big ball and cry!*

The train stopped again, this time pitching Elizabeth slightly forward in her seat. She looked up, startled, and saw a station with white tiled walls that read Prospect Park through the window.

*Prospect Park? Where's that?* Elizabeth wondered, twisting in her seat to look at the subway map mounted behind her on the wall. She located the D line and ran her finger farther and farther down until she found the stop.

Hot tears fell from Elizabeth's eyes. *I'm such an idiot!* she berated herself furiously. *How could I be this absentminded? I can't believe I got on the* downtown *train!* In her distress she must have boarded on the wrong platform. And now she was in the middle of Brooklyn—a huge and totally unfamiliar borough—headed straight for Coney Island.

Elizabeth buried her face in her hands and sobbed, her shoulders shaking uncontrollably. After the way her life had been all but turned upside down in the last twenty-four hours, it was the last straw. She felt utterly defeated and totally incapable of even trying to find her way back home.

"Production assistant—that sounds OK," Tom murmured as he circled the *Times* classified ad

156

heavily with his ballpoint pen. "Post-production assistant—that sounds OK too." He made another circle, set his pen down on the dining-room table, and reached for his glass of cranberry juice.

"Did you say something, Tom, dear?" Tish called from her room.

"Just thinking out loud," Tom called back, smiling. He was surprised by how glad he'd been to find Tish home when he'd staggered through the doorway and collapsed onto the couch. She had brought him water and vitamin C and brewed coriander while he took a cool shower and changed.

Tom turned back to the want ads and skimmed through a few more. In Tish's air-conditioned apartment, away from the crowded streets of Midtown and the danger of heatstroke, he was starting to feel much more relaxed. *Just because I didn't find a job today doesn't mean I'm totally hopeless,* Tom told himself as he took another sip of his juice.

Just then the phone rang, and Tom reached for the cordless. "Hello?"

"Tom?" Elizabeth sounded so choked up that it took him a split second to recognize her voice. "Tom, I'm so glad you're there!"

"Liz, where are you?" Tom was instantly on his feet, pacing with the phone. "What's wrong?"

"I—took—the—wrong—train," Elizabeth gasped between sobs.

"Liz, sweetheart, take a deep breath," Tom urged. "I'm listening. Just tell me where you are, and I'll come get you."

He heard Elizabeth let out a long, quavering

breath. "Coney Island," she said after a moment, in a more controlled voice. "Stillwell Avenue, at the end of the D line. How soon can you be here?"

"I'll get there as fast as I can," Tom promised. "Don't go anywhere. I love you, Liz."

He hung up the phone and checked his pockets to make sure he had his wallet and keys. "I'm going out to meet Liz," he yelled toward Tish's room as he ran out the door. "Back soon."

Tom's heart was pounding as he jogged up the street to Broadway. Elizabeth had sounded so distraught on the phone—he was terribly worried that something awful had happened to her. He was about to head down the stairs of the subway entrance when he suddenly thought better of it. Elizabeth had said she was at the end of the line; it would take him forever to get to her that way. If he hopped in a cab, it would cost a few dollars more, but the highways would get him to Elizabeth much quicker. The choice was clear.

*Liz needs me,* Tom told himself as he flagged down a taxi. *This is my chance to come through for her with flying colors!*

# Chapter Twelve

"Oh, boy, this *reeks!*" Jessica exclaimed as she held a huge soup cauldron at arm's length. "Did something curl up in here and *die?*"

As she and the other recruits scrubbed every inch of the mess hall's huge kitchen Jessica had remained more or less silent, trying not to call attention to herself. But the toxic odor of whatever was burned onto the soup pot had caught her off guard.

"If it did, they probably left it in the soup," Sunshine muttered from across the room where she was mopping the kitchen floor. "After all, roadkill chili is the cook's specialty. Right, Bev?"

"Right," the African American woman confirmed, her gaze directed at the sink she was scouring.

"For *real?*" Jessica squealed, her rubber-gloved arm frozen in midair. "I *ate* that chili at lunch!"

Bev snorted, shooting Jessica a contemptuous look over her shoulder. "Listen to Barbie. Do you *ever* take a joke?"

"As a matter of fact, I do, thank you very much," Jessica retorted. "I really enjoy whooping it up at my pink Malibu dream house. Any other highly original dumb-blonde remarks you want me to have a good laugh over?"

The second the words were out of her mouth, Jessica choked at how hostile her outburst had sounded. *They're going to rip me to shreds now for sure,* she lamented.

Bev tossed her scouring pad into the sink and turned to face Jessica. "Girl, you need to *chill.*" She chuckled, her eyes twinkling with amusement. "I was just playing—I know you're not the Barbie type. Not after the way you stood up to Pruitt."

"I admit, I thought you were like that at first," Sunshine chimed in from across the room. "But after you took care of that snake, I knew you were cool."

"But—but I don't get it!" Jessica exclaimed, floored. "I thought you guys hated me! Why were you laughing at me after the obstacle course?"

"Laughing at *you?*" The Filipina shook her curly ponytail adamantly. "We were laughing at *Pruitt.* Sunshine was telling us about the nasty stunt she pulled and how you guys got through the course anyway. We took one look at the expression on her face and cracked up. By the way, my name's Annette Polanco."

"Bev Vernon," Bev chimed in, playfully tipping the brim of her cap with exaggerated formality. "Charmed, my darling."

"Jessica Wakefield." Jessica beamed at her three new friends with relief and gratitude. "It's supernice

160

to meet you guys. You know, I was starting to worry that Pruitt had turned everybody against me."

"Are you kidding?" Bev scoffed. "Pruitt's about as popular around here as period cramps! If she hates you, that's a point in your favor."

"The only reason we go along with her is that nobody wants to get on her bad side," Annette added, nodding vigorously as she spoke.

Sunshine angrily threw her mop down on the floor. "What she pulled with us today was dirty, conniving, and underhanded," she declared, coming over to join them. "And sentencing *us* to KP duty just because *she* was humiliated that her little ploy failed—that was the icing on the cake."

She leaned against the wall and folded her arms across her chest, a stormy expression on her face. Jessica felt suddenly, intensely grateful that in crossing her, Pruitt had crossed Sunshine too. *Obviously she doesn't take any stuff from anyone, and neither do her friends,* Jessica thought admiringly. *I'm so glad they're on my side!*

"I don't know how she gets away with it," Annette agreed, peeling off her rubber gloves and stepping away from the sink. "She's such a *witch*, with her beady little eyes and her mouth all pursed like she was sucking a lemon."

"OK, *thank* you," Jessica said righteously, gesturing at Annette as if she had just proved a point of Jessica's. "A few dots of undereye concealer and some lip liner could do that woman a *world* of good."

"She's *beyond* help," Bev asserted, waving her

arm dismissively. "She makes the creepy-crawly things in the swamp look like supermodels."

Sunshine's angry expression melted into one of glee. "Have you ever seen her without her cap on? I *swear* she has a bald spot. She needs to join the Hair Club for Uptight Women."

Jessica erupted into giggles along with Annette and Bev. Looking satisfied, Sunshine reached into the breast pocket of her uniform and extracted a cigar.

Bev rested the palms of her hands on the countertop and boosted herself onto it. "I believe it," she affirmed. "Her hair is so greasy, it probably slides right out of its sockets."

"Follicles," Annette corrected.

"Whatever," Bev said with a dismissive wave of her hand. "Either way, Pruitt is *u-g-l-y*."

"Her skin looks like the stuff that's caked onto this nasty soup tureen," Jessica said, staring ruefully at the burned crust. "She needs, like, a Brillo facial."

Sunshine laughed so hard that she sucked in a mouthful of cigar smoke and had a coughing fit, which made the others laugh even harder. Jessica grinned, her heart warmed by the sense of solidarity that only a common enemy could invoke. *Things are definitely going to be different now that Sunshine and her friends have my back!* she thought with satisfaction.

*I'm on my way, Liz,* Tom telegraphed mentally as the cab sped down Broadway. He was so anxious to get to Elizabeth that he almost felt grateful for the way New York cabbies drove at breakneck speed.

The driver made a sudden sharp left, sending Tom flying across the backseat and leaving the pit of his stomach on the other side. He groped for his seat belt with trembling fingers and clicked the buckle into place, pushing his fears for his own well-being out of his mind. He had to keep it together for Elizabeth's sake.

*Please, let her be OK*, he prayed silently as the cab rumbled over a pothole. *I'll never forgive myself if anything happens to her!*

The more anxious Tom felt, the more guilt crept into the pit of his stomach. In a way he would be partially to blame if Elizabeth had gotten herself into a dangerous situation. After all, he was the one pushing her to take risks and try new experiences while she was in New York.

*Granted,* I *meant the kind of experiences you have in the safety of your own bedroom,* Tom allowed. But what if Elizabeth had felt so much pressure that she'd gone and done something rash? There were any number of horrible things that could happen to a beautiful young woman alone in the city—especially one as friendly and trusting as Elizabeth Wakefield. Tom felt sick at the thought of anyone taking advantage of her kindness.

*Don't think about it,* Tom commanded himself. *Just concentrate on Liz.*

He ran over the events of last night in his mind, remembering the confusion that had clouded Elizabeth's blue-green eyes during their conversation at the Empire State Building. *Had* he put too much pressure on her? He'd tried to reassure her that he would wait as long as she wanted him to . . . but it was hard to hide the depth of his desire for her. Elizabeth had to know that living this close to her, on the verge of intimacy beyond anything they'd shared before, was driving him slowly insane.

For a moment, as he relaxed into the rolling motion of the taxi, Tom was lost in the memory of their passionate cab ride the night before. He flashed back to Elizabeth's flushed face, her tousled golden hair . . . to the way her hands and lips had searched hungrily for his. It certainly didn't *seem* as if she was feeling pressured—in fact, Tom was almost positive she'd wanted him as much as he wanted her. But obviously something was still holding her back.

*I can understand if she's scared,* Tom acknowledged as he gazed out the window. They had crossed the bridge into Brooklyn, leaving the towering skyscrapers of Manhattan behind. *When it comes to sex, women definitely have a lot more to take into consideration than men do.*

But still, Tom had let her know time and time again that they were in this together; that he would be there for her no matter what. *It's not like I'm some sleazeball who's planning to ditch Liz as soon as I get what I want!* he reminded himself. After all, he'd followed her all the way to New York. If that didn't show Elizabeth how committed he was, Tom didn't know *what* would.

*It's so frustrating,* Tom thought with a low groan. *Doesn't she realize everything I went through to be with her? You'd think* she *would want to do something for* me!

Suddenly the taxi screeched to an abrupt halt, as if Tom's thoughts had somehow derailed its momentum. With a start he shook himself back to reality.

*What am I* thinking? Tom berated himself, running his hands through his hair in anguished exasperation. *I don't want Liz to make love* for *me. I want her to make love* with *me! My coming to New York has zero to do with her choice—and only a* dog *would think otherwise*.

The driver swung his head around. "Coney Island," he announced. "That'll be sixty bucks."

*"What?"*

"Thanks so much for coming to get me, Tom." Elizabeth smiled up at her boyfriend as they strolled hand in hand down the Coney Island boardwalk. "I feel a lot better now that you're here. I guess I overreacted about getting on the wrong train."

"Don't be silly." Tom leaned down to kiss her hair. "You were alone in a strange city, and you got lost. It's totally understandable."

Elizabeth felt herself flush. On the quaint, picturesque boardwalk, with the seashore on one side and amusement park rides on the other, the stresses of the city seemed a million miles away. She breathed in the fresh, early evening sea breeze and sighed.

"Maybe if I was *eleven*," she conceded sheepishly. "But once you turn eighteen, you're not really supposed to burst into tears every time you take a wrong turn."

Tom grinned and squeezed her hand. "Don't sweat it. Everyone grows up at their own pace."

Elizabeth met Tom's eyes. *Is he talking about last night?* she wondered. *How I almost decided to "grow up" and then changed my mind?* But on Tom's face she read only love and open relief.

*Tom really* was *worried about me,* Elizabeth realized, her heart overflowing with love as they walked past an ancient wooden roller coaster overgrown with ivy. *Whenever I need him, he drops everything. How many girls are lucky enough to have an actual knight in shining armor?*

"You're really wonderful, you know that?" she asked Tom. "I don't know what I would do without you."

In response Tom planted a kiss on her lips, stopping them both in their tracks. It began as a quick peck, but when he drew away, Elizabeth surprised herself by grabbing his collar and pulling him back toward her. They kissed again, broke apart, and then came together again, like two magnets irresistibly drawn to each other's force.

Finally Elizabeth managed to pull away, exhaling deeply to quiet the pounding of her heart. *What's gotten into me?* she chided herself. They were standing not three yards away from a family of five seated on a bench eating ice-cream cones.

All at once she felt light-headed, and not just from the kisses. Elizabeth's mind and heart were doing flip-flops at the rate of a mile a minute. *All day I've been telling myself how insane I was to even consider jumping into bed with Tom,* she mused.

166

*But now that we're together, I can't take my hands off him!*

"Wow," Tom gasped as they resumed walking. "Don't take this the wrong way, Liz, but you should get lost more often."

"Watch it, pal." Elizabeth giggled playfully. "I feel ridiculous enough without you teasing me."

The smile drained from her face as she flashed back to the mortifying scene at the theater. "I wouldn't have gotten lost in the first place if Gerald and Claire hadn't been so cruel. They made me feel like my play was worse than one of those Thanksgiving pageants you put on in third grade."

"Who cares about what those two idiots think?" Tom slipped a consoling arm around her shoulders and leaned his head on hers. His nearness sent a delicious shiver down Elizabeth's spine. "Remember, you were picked for the same honor they were. Your work is as good as theirs or, more likely, better."

"But Ted agreed with them!" Elizabeth protested, frowning as she remembered the awkward silence that had greeted her reading. "He had a million notes for me—I don't know how I'm supposed to rework the script."

"I'm sure you're up to the challenge," Tom assured her, squeezing her shoulder. "The Elizabeth Wakefield I know has never shied away from a tough assignment."

Elizabeth brightened at his words. *He really is the perfect boyfriend,* she thought as she gazed at him adoringly. *He always knows just what to say when I'm stressing about my work. He actually values my mind as much as my body.* Plus he looked incredibly handsome in his faded blue pocket tee and brown corduroys, and he smelled great—soap-and-water fresh, like he'd just taken a shower. *Too bad I'm not exactly respecting him for* his *mind right now!* Elizabeth added mischievously.

"What?" Tom stopped walking. "What are you smiling about? You look like the cat that ate the canary."

Speechless, Elizabeth met Tom's gaze. For a moment their eyes locked intensely. She felt almost as if electricity were visibly crackling in the air between them. His arm was around her, and their faces were so close. Elizabeth was aching to kiss him . . . but she didn't want to initiate another PDA.

Blushing, she looked away. The sky over the ocean was beginning to turn pink and purple. The white lights of the carnival rides twinkled brightly in the dusk. It was a romantic, almost magical scene. But all of a sudden Elizabeth had the overwhelming urge to be at home . . . with Tom . . . behind closed doors.

"You know," Elizabeth began, "I'm getting kind of tired. Do you want to head back soon?"

"Sure, Liz," Tom said in a low voice that suggested he knew what was on her mind. "Let's get going. But do you mind if we take the subway? That cab ride pretty much cleaned me out."

"Fine," Elizabeth said absently, her stomach

twisting with nervous anticipation. Part of her couldn't wait to get back to the apartment—and the rest of her was terrified of what would happen when and if her hormones took over.

"Anybody home?" Tom called out into the silence of the darkened apartment. "Tish, you there?"

There was no response. Elizabeth stooped to switch on a table lamp that had been draped with a gauzy yellow scarf. Soft amber light flooded the room.

"Look, she left a note," Elizabeth observed as she straightened up. Tom followed her gaze to a sheet of white paper that lay on the dining-room table. He walked over and picked it up.

Hi, kids!
    Gone to the Aquarius Dawn seminar on alternative spirituality. Back late—don't wait up. Soybean casserole in fridge can be heated in microwave, three minutes on high.
                                    Love, Tish

Tom barely registered the end of the note; the words *back late* were reverberating in his mind, reflecting infinite possibilities.

"Looks like we have the place to ourselves," Tom said casually, trying not to let his jubilation show in his voice. He folded the note and put it back on the table. "There's a casserole in the fridge if we want it. Are you hungry?"

Elizabeth shook her head wordlessly, not taking her eyes from his face. *Is she thinking what I'm thinking?* Tom wondered. *And if she is, is she as excited about it as I am?*

"Neither am I," he replied, taking a step toward Elizabeth. "At least," he added softly, "not for casserole."

Elizabeth stood by the lamp and shifted her weight from one foot to the other as if she didn't quite know what to do with herself. Tom had the urge to press her body to his in a powerful, protective embrace. But instead he drew slowly toward her, reaching out to run a finger down the side of her arm. Elizabeth shivered slightly, then reached up and wrapped her arms around Tom's neck.

"Alone at last," he murmured throatily, overcome with emotion as he encircled her slender waist with his arms. "You look so beautiful, Liz. Like an angel."

"Oh, Tom," Elizabeth whispered as her body relaxed against his. Tom could hear his heart beating in time with Elizabeth's. But otherwise everything was perfectly still, as if frozen in time. His gaze took in Elizabeth's sparkling blue-green eyes, her rosebud lips. He wanted to savor this exquisite moment for as long as he could . . . but at the same time he had a feeling things were about to move further. A *lot* further.

"Please tell me you love me as much as I love you," he said quietly, leaning toward her.

"I love you," Elizabeth responded immediately,

but her words were swallowed up by his kiss.

In an instant they were locked in a furious embrace. Tom felt Elizabeth's fingertips running through his hair, then raking down his back. He could scarcely believe he was here, alone with Elizabeth in the heat of passion, without Tish, crazy cabdrivers, or anything else to distract them.

*Tonight's the night!* Tom exulted to himself. *I just know it!*

"Mmmm," Elizabeth murmured. She closed her eyes and leaned back languidly on the couch as Tom traced a fiery line of kisses from her neck to her collarbone. "That feels so nice."

"You like that?" Tom's voice was low and husky; she could feel his face next to hers. "How's *this?*"

Elizabeth opened her eyes in time to see him gently lift a lock of golden hair off her neck. As he began nibbling on her earlobe a delicious warm tingle spread through her from the tips of her toes to her scalp. Elizabeth closed her eyes again. "Wonderful," she sighed blissfully.

For a moment she allowed herself to be swept away by the exquisite sensation of Tom's mouth on her skin. Then from a distant place in the back of her mind, almost from outside herself, Elizabeth felt the distant stirrings of worry. Tom's kisses were amazing, but everything was happening so fast. She barely even recalled how they had ended up on the couch.

*It's obvious he wants things to go further tonight . . . but is that what I want?* Elizabeth wasn't sure, but she knew she had to decide—and soon. She could hardly hear herself think over the blood rushing in her ears.

Tom's lips reached hers, and they were instantly locked in a passionate, all-consuming kiss. In spite of the air-conditioning Elizabeth's body felt as if it were on fire. Her heart was thudding so loudly that she half expected Tish's neighbors to call and complain. She could feel the intensity of their desire for each other building by the second.

"I love you so much, Liz," Tom whispered when they came up for air. Tenderly he traced the line of her cheekbone with his fingertip. "I can't tell you how happy I am right now."

*Would he still be happy if I said no?* Elizabeth wondered achingly as Tom's mouth trailed more soft kisses down her neck.

*Maybe we* should *just take the plunge,* she reasoned, her body turning to jelly in Tom's arms. *After all, we love each other, and I can't imagine making love for the first time with anyone else.*

Just then Elizabeth felt Tom fumbling with the buttons on her oxford shirt. One came undone, and his fingers slid down to the next one. Elizabeth's eyes flew open in alarm, and she glanced down to see a swell of white lace bra peeking out of her shirt. Goose bumps prickled on her exposed skin.

*OK, so we're going to do it,* she told herself as she closed her eyes and tried to relax back into Tom's kisses. *It's no big deal. Tom's the perfect boyfriend. He's done so much for me. . . . I might as well just do this for him.*

Suddenly Elizabeth pieced together what she had just thought. Her eyes flew open, and she jerked bolt upright on the couch, gathering her unbuttoned shirt around her with her hands. *What's wrong with you?* Elizabeth asked herself furiously. *You actually considered having sex with Tom because he* wanted *it, not you! Don't even* think *about making love out of guilt. You don't "owe" him anything!*

"Liz, what's wrong?" Tom stared at her with an expression that was part puzzled and part crushed. "Did I cross a line? I'm so sorry, Liz—I honestly thought you were into it."

Elizabeth felt her face flame beet red. She had let things go too far, and now that she saw Tom's confused, puppy-dog look, she was horrified with herself.

"No, it's not that," she assured him hastily as she fumbled with her buttons. "I—I just have a . . . a lot of work to do on my play."

"On your play," Tom repeated in a dumbfounded tone.

"Yes, my play," Elizabeth confirmed, hearing her voice falter only slightly. "I just have so many revisions to make—I'm really getting stressed out about it. I can't concentrate on anything else right now."

When Tom winced, she hastened to add, "I didn't mean I *wasn't* concentrating. I was—I mean . . . it was incredible—you're always incredible—I just . . ." She sighed and shrugged helplessly. "Tom, you know how it is when you have an important broadcast coming up. This is live theater,

173

and I'm totally inexperienced. I really don't want to embarrass myself."

Tom silently searched her face as if he were trying to decide which kind of "inexperience" she was really worried about. Finally he nodded. "OK, Liz. If you have to work, you have to work. But you know where I am if you change your mind."

"Thanks, Tom." Elizabeth threw her arms around his neck for a brief, awkward hug, pulled back, and got to her feet. "I knew you would understand. You're the sweetest boyfriend a girl could ever have."

*But that's no reason to rush into bed with you before I'm ready,* she added silently as she picked up her backpack and headed for her room.

*There's* nothing *here I'm qualified for,* Tom thought as he turned another page of the want ads defeatedly. The rustle of the newspaper seemed to fill the bedroom.

Tom leaned back against his pillows and heaved a lonely sigh. He was beginning to think *nothing* was going to go his way while he was in New York. Not only was he jobless and totally devoid of prospects, he had ended up in bed alone . . . *again.*

*I was so sure tonight was the night,* Tom reflected ruefully. Elizabeth's body language had given him nothing but green lights. Not in a million years would Tom have guessed that while *he* thought they were locked in one of their hottest clinches ever, *she* was thinking about her script. Now he'd all but given up on trying to read Elizabeth's signals.

*Liz could walk into this room right now wearing nothing but a huge red bow, and I'd still think she'd change her mind,* he thought glumly.

Tom let the newspaper fall onto the bedspread and rubbed his eyes wearily with his palms. He was trying so hard to be the perfect boyfriend, to be understanding and patient. And he was trying *especially* hard not to take Elizabeth's abrupt brush-off personally. *The whole reason we're in New York is because of Liz's play,* Tom reminded himself. *Obviously she has work to do. It doesn't mean she's not interested in our relationship.*

Still, it was tough to understand how Elizabeth could be so immune to all his attempts at seduction. Not only had he come through for her at every turn, from Sweet Valley to Coney Island, but also he had moved at her pace and been sensitive to her needs. *What did I do wrong?* Tom berated himself. *What more can I do to convince Liz that the time is right?*

Suddenly he had the uncomfortable feeling he was being watched. When he looked up, Tom noticed a classical-Greek-styled plaster bust on the dresser. It was of a stern, bearded man—probably Plato or Socrates or somebody—glaring at him almost reproachfully, as if he knew what Tom was thinking about. Tom felt the skin on the back of his neck prickle; it was creepy to have someone in the room staring at him even if it was only someone made of stone. *Why couldn't Diane have posters of rock stars on her walls, like a* normal *college student?* Tom wondered, all at once feeling like a stranger in what was supposed to be his own room.

With a pang he recalled the modest but cozy apartment he'd had to give up in Sweet Valley, with its charming little garden and bubbling stream. Maybe it wasn't as spacious and ideally located as Tish's place, but it had been *his*. Staying there all summer without Elizabeth had seemed totally unthinkable . . . but now, even though only a wall separated them, Tom felt as distanced from his girlfriend as if he'd stayed in California.

It wasn't that he didn't love and support Elizabeth. And it certainly wasn't that he was only in New York to, as his old football buddies would say, "get some action." But when he thought about what he'd sacrificed to be with her—his apartment in Sweet Valley and especially his internship in L.A. . . .

*Don't even go there,* Tom ordered himself, picking up the want ads and tossing them to the ground in frustration. *If you keep dwelling on what you gave up, you're going to go completely insane.*

Tom switched off the light by the nightstand and burrowed under the covers, feeling profoundly exhausted. His mind had been spinning in circles for hours. *Just let things wind down a bit,* he told himself. *Remember, tomorrow's another day.*

# Chapter
# Thirteen

"Nice of you to join us, Wakefield." Sergeant Pruitt snorted as Jessica brought up the rear of a line of recruits. "Spend a little less time on your *makeup*, and you might actually make it to breakfast on time."

"Get bent, Pruneface," Jessica muttered under her breath as she joined the cluster of women standing on the sidelines of the practice field. It wasn't because of her makeup that she had been late to breakfast—it was because she physically *couldn't* get out of bed at 6 A.M. Jessica didn't see how the recruits could be expected to wake up at so ludicrous an hour on Tuesday after spending all Monday doing strenuous exercises.

*At least I don't have to actually* do *anything at this exercise,* Jessica reflected, shielding her eyes with her hand as she surveyed the line of torso-shaped targets arranged in a row on the field. Only the recruits who had experience with automatic firearms would be participating in target practice; the others were expected to observe in preparation for their own training later. When Pruitt had announced the exercise last night, Jessica felt mildly disappointed that she wouldn't be in on the action, but now she was relieved to have a break.

"Hey, girlfriend." Annette came up beside her and fanned her face with her hand. "Hot enough for you?"

"Ugh—no question." Jessica plucked at her sleeves, which were sticking to her skin. The rain had finally cleared, but the air was still thick and heavy with humidity and haze. "I'm used to heat, but at least California is *dry*. I can feel my pores clogging as we speak."

Annette gave her a light slap on the arm. "Oh, stop. I bet you've never had a zit a day in your life. Hey, isn't that your friend over there?"

Jessica could barely make out a broad, muscular figure silhouetted by the shimmering sunlight. She put her hand to her brow and squinted, bringing Harlan's features into place. He was standing apart from the other recruits waiting for the targets, and he had unbuttoned his uniform to the waist, revealing a white ribbed tank top that clung tightly to his sweaty, muscular body.

Annette whistled. "Girl, he is *fine*."

"No doubt." Jessica nodded trancelike without tearing her eyes from Harlan. She was dimly aware of the blasts of gunfire in the distance.

As she watched, Harlan shrugged off the sleeves of his uniform shirt and tied them around his waist.

His bare shoulders and well-defined arms gleamed with perspiration. To Jessica he looked like a Greek god who had descended from the sky, or at least from a diet Coke ad.

"*Yum,*" she declared to Annette, who giggled conspiratorily.

Just then Harlan appeared to notice Jessica eyeing his bod. He met her gaze, grinned, and winked as if to let her know he enjoyed the attention. Jessica blushed and looked away.

"Ogle much?" Bev asked, coming up between Jessica and Annette and slinging an arm around each of them.

"You guys didn't even hear us sneaking up behind you," Sunshine added, appearing at Annette's elbow. "I'm sure you'll make *great* agents."

"I *will* make a great agent," Jessica retorted. "I never take my eyes off a target."

She couldn't help staring while Harlan positioned himself before the practice target As he cocked his gun he glanced over at Jessica and raised his eyebrow as if to say, *Get a load of me.* He turned to the target, braced his legs in a wide, swaggering stance, and proceeded to fire off rounds frenetically.

In seconds the target was hanging in tattered shards on its metal frame, but Harlan kept on firing until he apparently had no ammo left. He turned around, shouldered his gun, and flexed his bicep before looking straight at Jessica and wiggling his eyebrows.

"Who does that guy think he is, the Terminator?" Sunshine snorted. "Is he *kidding?*"

"I don't think so," Jessica said flatly. "Eew, what a cheeseball! I mean, he's really hot and everything, but puh-*leeze*, that macho ego stuff is *such* a turnoff."

Suddenly an all-too-familiar whistle pierced the air. "Cease fire! *Wakefield!*"

Jessica's knees turned to Jell-O. "Uh-oh!" she moaned. "Pruitt's after me *again!* What have I done *now?*"

"OK, Tim." Gerald clapped imperiously. "I want to see you confront the apple. Really *confront* it. Really engage in the struggle between eros and Thanatos—those two conflicting primal urges toward lust and death. I want to *see* that struggle on your face." Gerald's eyelids fluttered shut for a moment as if he were rhapsodized by his own words.

"It's Jim," explained the actor onstage, an NYU film student in a flannel shirt, jeans, and an incongruous multicolored jester's hat that Gerald had insisted he wear for effect. "My name is Jim."

Gerald's eyes snapped open. *"Whatever,"* he hissed. "Action!"

Jim began struggling visibly for an appropriate expression. As his head nodded and twitched, the bells on his jester hat jingled. "I feel society's knife through my heart!" he squeaked after a sidelong glance at the script in his hand.

From her seat in the front row of the main stage area, Elizabeth let out a low sigh as she wondered how many more hapless actors Gerald was going to drive off the stage. Already two prospective male

180

leads had dashed the jester's hat to the floorboards in frustration and stalked away. The sparse "audience" in the Maxwell's seats, including Ted, Claire, and the cast Claire had just chosen for her play, was growing restless as Gerald tortured actor after actor.

Elizabeth was starting to worry that by the time Gerald finished casting his play, all the actors who had showed up to try out for *her* play would be gone. Gerald's auditions had already lasted over an hour and a half, while Claire had wrapped hers up in less than an hour. The handsome young guy Elizabeth had met outside the theater Monday was the first to try out, and Claire had cast him instantly. Elizabeth had been secretly hoping that Claire would reject him for not being weird or affected enough—the guy would have been perfect for the part of Gavin in *Two Sides to Every Story.* But obviously Claire wasn't so far off in her own world that she couldn't recognize talent.

"Cut!" Gerald shrieked, clapping again. "That's *pathos,* not *eros!* And your attempt at *Thanatos* is woefully reminiscent of *bathos.* Are you trying to drive me *insane?*"

Jim looked as if he was about to cry. "No, I just . . . I'm sorry, but I don't understand the terms you're using. Would you mind just explaining my motivation?" he pleaded. "Or . . . or is there any background information on the character that I might be able to use?"

*"Motivation?"* Gerald sneered. "Of all the trite—"

"Maybe you could just work with what *you* get from the script, Jim," Elizabeth interjected hurriedly, hoping to defuse Gerald's anger before he totally crushed the young actor's ego. "I'm sure if you just read the lines in a way that expresses your natural reaction to them, you'll do fine."

Jim looked grateful. But when she glanced over at Gerald and met his gaze, Elizabeth gulped. He was practically turning purple. His temples throbbed and his eyes blazed.

"*Excuse* me, Elizabeth," Gerald spat in an indignant, contemptuous tone, his voice echoing through the almost empty theater. "If I recall correctly, there were quite a few issues with your 'play' that needed to be addressed." When he said the word *play*, Gerald lifted his hands and curled his fingers into sarcastic quotation marks. "Perhaps you should think about solving *your* problems first."

Hot tears sprang to Elizabeth's eyes. *I can't believe he did that in front of everyone!* she thought as anger and humiliation washed over her in vicious waves. With shaking hands Elizabeth smoothed down the long skirt of her blue-and-white floral-print sundress. Then she jumped up out of her seat, grabbed her backpack, and walked quickly out of the theater on wobbly legs.

As soon as she reached the lobby Elizabeth's walk turned to a run. Blinded by tears, she managed to stumble her way out of the building, weeping uncontrollably.

*I'm just not cut out for the theater,* Elizabeth realized as she headed for the subway. *Fellowship or no*

182

*fellowship, I can't take these personal attacks. I'm quitting!*

"So once you're reunited with your ex, what do you want to say to him?" Jenny Tracey asked, her glossy red lips tight with feigned concern.

The camera panned to a woman dressed in a neon green Lycra dress and fishnet stockings who was nervously clutching a single red rose. "I want to tell him that my baby is not really his—it was conceived during my alien abduction," she confessed. "Even if he can't forgive me, I'm willing to give our relationship another chance."

"Where do they *get* these people?" Tom muttered, flopping back on the couch and shaking his head in disbelief. He couldn't believe some of the freaks who paraded their sordid lives on *Tease-n-Tell*. He'd never seen such a sickening mockery of broadcast journalism in his life. But then again, *he* was the loser with nothing better to do than sit at home watching it.

Tom reached down and picked up the nearest crumpled newspaper. He halfheartedly scanned the heavily marked-up want ads just in case he'd missed something, but he'd already called about every job that was remotely within his field of experience—all with zero results.

*It's hopeless,* he told himself. *Unless someone decides to pay me to sit around watching trashy talk shows, I have no job opportunities whatsoever.*

"I Have a Startling Revelation!" Tom declared aloud, echoing *Tease-n-Tell*'s topic of the day. "I have no life, I'm a complete and total failure, and my girlfriend despises me!"

"Did you say something, dear?" Tish suddenly materialized in the doorway of her bedroom. "Is anything wrong?"

Tom sat up and reached for the remote control. "No, no—everything's fine," he assured her sheepishly as he switched off *Tease-n-Tell.* "I was just, uh, feeling sorry for myself. I'm kind of stressed out since I haven't been able to find work yet."

Tish fluttered her arms in the air, causing her clunky wooden bracelets to clatter. Her salt-and-pepper hair was flowing loose, and she was wearing a white crocheted skullcap and a flowing turquoise silk pantsuit. "In that case I have an offer to make you!" she exclaimed. "I have a few aromatherapy clients coming over today, but my assistant called in sick—she was experiencing some disturbance in her aura. If you're not busy, would you mind filling in for her? I could compensate you at the end of the day with one of my stress-release herbal treatments—they really bring clarity and help you get past your anxieties."

"Aromatherapy? Me? Well, I don't know anything about it, but . . ." *Could I really keep a straight face about all that New Age stuff?* he wondered. *Then again, a little humor might take my mind off my problems . . . and it's a lot better than moping around all day.*

"Why not?" Tom agreed with an affable shrug. "It's the least I can do after all the generosity you've shown us. And if there's one thing I could use right now, it's a stress-release treatment."

"Organizing another semiformal, princess?" Sergeant Pruitt curled her thin lips into a cruel, mocking sneer. "I *warned* you about fraternizing—I will *not* have you causing disruptions among the other recruits. This time you get forty laps around the field!" Her bony finger pointed toward a wide circle of track about a hundred yards from the target practice range.

"But I *wasn't* fraternizing!" Jessica protested. "We were all just watching like we were supposed to!"

"Yeah," Bev chimed in. "Wakefield wasn't disrupting anything—we were *all* talking while we watched the practice."

"Singling her out is totally bogus," Annette agreed while Sunshine just glowered.

"*Bogus,* huh? Is that so?" The muscles in Pruitt's neck twitched. "Well, let me rectify this injustice immediately. You're *all* charged with fraternizing! Forty laps for each of you—now *march!*"

Jessica exchanged looks with her friends and saw in their eyes the same helpless outrage she felt. Tossing her hair over her shoulder, she threw back her head and stalked toward the field, feeling Pruitt's eyes boring into her back. Sunshine and the others followed closely on Jessica's heels.

"I'm supersorry, you guys," Jessica said as soon as they were out of earshot. "I really appreciate you sticking up for me and all, but I didn't want you to get in trouble."

"Don't sweat it," Bev answered glibly. "It's not your fault that Pruitt's a vengeful witch."

"Yeah," Sunshine agreed, breaking into a jog as they reached the course. "She just looks for excuses to make people's lives a living hell."

The thick, humid air made it hard to run and breathe, so for a while they jogged without talking, hearing nothing but the gun blasts in the distance. As Jessica circled the course she ceased to be aware of anything but the strain of moving her legs through the heat.

"Hey, look!" Annette cried suddenly, breaking Jessica out of her concentration. "They're wrapping it up over at the target practice. I don't see Pruitt anywhere, do you?"

Jessica turned her head to see that only a few straggling figures remained by the targets. "No, I don't see her," Jessica said hesitantly, slowing to a walk.

"Well, I don't hear that damn whistle going off every five seconds," Bev pointed out. "So it looks like we're on our own."

"Freedom!" Sunshine cheered before she stopped running and hunched over to catch her breath.

"She's not going to come back here and check on us." Bev slowed her pace and veered toward Sunshine. "Remember how she was yelling about having a meeting with FSSA top brass right after target practice? I say we get *out* of here."

"But where would we go?" Jessica asked as she hobbled over. She was less than thrilled about the prospect of finishing her forty laps, but she didn't feel safe prancing around the compound in full view of Pruitt's meeting.

"Well, we *could* go see you-know-who." Bev elbowed Annette in the ribs and winked. "I'm *dying* to meet him."

"*Stop!*" Annette squealed, blushing. "Quit teasing me. I wish I'd never told you about Al."

"Al?" Jessica asked, confused.

"The boxing instructor." Sunshine lit a cigar. "Annette's got a big old crush on him."

"I do *not!*" Annette protested. A sneaky grin spread across her pretty face. "I just have a little teensy one. But the gym *is* pretty secluded. I doubt Pruitt would find us there. Wanna go for it?"

"I'm game." Bev bounced up and down impatiently. "Come on, let's go!"


"Elizabeth! Elizabeth, wait!"

Through a blur of tears Elizabeth turned and saw the young man she'd met on her first day at the Maxwell— the one Claire had cast as her lead. He was running down the street toward her, concern on his handsome face.

She wiped the tears from her cheeks. "How did you know my name?" she demanded.

"I heard old Tennessee Williams back there call you Elizabeth," the guy confessed, deadpan. "Sorry if I startled you, but I couldn't let you run off like that. If you ask me, the producer is a real jerk for letting that pretentious twerp talk to you like that. Anyway, I just wanted you to know that there was at least *one* human being with feelings in that theater."

Elizabeth felt a fresh round of tears spring to her eyes. "I appreciate the thought—I really do— but I'm not sure *one* nice person is enough to keep me sane." Too embarrassed to meet his eyes, she stared at the ground and shook her head. "I just don't think I'm cut out for this dog-eat-dog stuff. I'm going to hand Ted my letter of resignation tomorrow."

"Are you kidding? You can't quit!" The actor sounded genuinely shocked. "Do you have any idea how many people would love to be in your shoes right now?"

"I guess," Elizabeth said, feeling a twinge of guilt. When he put it that way, quitting *did* seem like a cop-out.

"I'll tell you something, Elizabeth," the young man said solemnly. "It's a common misconception that the theater is a supportive environment with sensitive, caring people. Believe it or not, you actually need a pretty thick skin to survive."

To her own surprise, Elizabeth burst out laughing. "OK, OK, I get your point," she conceded, dabbing at her eyes with a knuckle. "Maybe I *am* overreacting."

"Not at all! Theater people *need* to make their emotions larger than life." He winked playfully. "Seriously, I don't blame you for getting upset. It *is* a big challenge to keep your head screwed on straight around some of these inflated egos. But if you tough it out, you'll prove something important to yourself."

Elizabeth took a deep breath. "You're right,"

she agreed. "I didn't come all the way from California to quit after one day. My pride was hurt, so I just lost perspective for a minute. Come on, let's go back." When she started walking toward the Maxwell, the actor fell into step beside her.

"Thanks a lot for coming to talk to me," Elizabeth said as they approached the theater. "It really helped, uh . . . I'm sorry, I don't even know your name!"

"It's Vince," he supplied. "Nice to meet you, Elizabeth."

Elizabeth looked over at Vince and felt as if a lightbulb had gone on over her head. *It's Vince* Klee, *the movie star!* she thought excitedly. *That's why I connected him with Jessica—she has his poster on her wall. He looks so much shorter in person!*

"My sister would *kill* me if she knew I was standing here talking to you!" Elizabeth breathed, feeling incredibly silly for having bawled her eyes out in front of a movie star. "I can't believe I didn't recognize you."

Vince grinned and rolled his eyes. "I know, I seem really short, right?"

Elizabeth giggled nervously. "So, what made a movie star like you decide to try out for a student production?" she asked, avoiding his question.

"Um, it embarrasses me deeply to say this," Vince admitted, scratching his head sheepishly, "but some critics have called me . . . a pretty boy."

Elizabeth couldn't suppress a smile. "That's terrible."

"Well, personally I don't really see the 'pretty' thing," Vince went on, "but what bothers me more is the assumption that I'm a one-dimensional actor. So my agent suggested I do some theater to challenge myself *and* beef up my credibility. He told me this production gets a lot of local press, and Claire's play was something edgy and avant-garde—a real risky move for me."

*That's one way of putting it,* Elizabeth thought wryly. "So you're here to prove something to yourself," she observed. "I think that's really brave of you."

Vince smiled as he held open the door of the Maxwell. "Well, Elizabeth, I think *you're* pretty brave too."

"Hey, Al!" Annette called. "Can we come in?"

Jessica followed Annette into the gym with the others. At the back of the room a bronzed, buff guy was lifting barbells on a bench near a row of punching bags. "Annette!" he cried, replacing the barbell and sliding his body out from underneath it. "Yeah, come in! And who are these lovely ladies?"

As Al sat up and wiped the sweat from his brow Jessica saw that he was a handsome young Latino with big brown eyes and a close-cropped beard. *Cute, very cute,* Jessica thought admiringly. *But Annette saw him first.*

"Al, these are my friends: Sunshine, Bev, and Jessica," Annette introduced. "We're escaping from Pruitt. Mind if we hide out here for a few?"

"Of course not!" Al grinned broadly, his eyes sparkling.

*I bet Annette's feelings are totally mutual*, Jessica speculated. *That guy looks totally love struck!*

Sunshine had wandered over to the punching bags and was thumping them experimentally with the side of her fist. "Hey, Al, how about giving us a lesson?" she called. "I've got a lot of aggression that I wouldn't mind getting out right now."

"That's what I'm here for!" Al agreed cheerfully, rising to his feet. "Let's get you set up. Gloves are in the equipment locker right behind you."

In a few minutes Jessica and her friends had been laced into their gloves. Jessica felt a little foolish with huge padded blobs protruding from her arms, but when she tentatively bopped the punching bag, she was surprised by how much power she felt in her enormous "fist."

"OK, stand with your feet shoulder width apart," Al instructed, placing his hands on Annette's hips to illustrate. Jessica and Bev exchanged knowing looks as they adjusted their positions. "Now start bouncing from foot to foot. Jab out with one arm. . . . Yeah, that's it."

Jessica struck out at the punching bag with all her might, imagining that she was delivering blows directly to Pruitt's face. The bag swung jerkily back and forth as she rained punches on it. *This is pretty cool*, Jessica decided as she pictured Pruitt reeling.

"Don't swing to the side, Annette—jab straight out, like this." Al stopped sparring with Annette and came up behind her to straighten her arm. He

191

glanced over at Jessica. "Check out your friend Jessica—her stance is *perfect*."

"What's your secret, Wakefield?" Annette asked teasingly.

Jessica narrowed her eyes at her mentally projected picture of Pruitt and delivered a forceful uppercut to its jaw. "Visualization," she replied.

# Chapter
# Fourteen

"Somebody doesn't *want* us to discover the truth, my love. They're willing to stop at nothing—maybe even murder—to sweep this scandal under the rug. And I don't want to see you get hurt, Phoebe. So I'm taking you off the story!"

"Thanks, Ken, I think I've seen enough." Elizabeth smiled up at the sandy-haired young man standing alone onstage. "You seem to have a feel for Gavin. You've got the part."

"Wow, thanks!" Ken Deal stepped down from the stage and flashed a warm, open grin that made Elizabeth feel positive he was the right choice for her male lead.

Ken took a seat in the audience, and Elizabeth turned her mind to the process of casting Phoebe. She was reviewing the pile of head shots and resumes attached to her clipboard when she heard Ted calling her name.

"Elizabeth! You won't believe the coup I've

scored! Your leading lady has *arrived!*" Ted hurried toward her, his hands hovering protectively around the shoulders of a short, eccentrically dressed woman. "Elizabeth, may I introduce Hildy Muldman," he announced, bowing with a dramatic flourish. "Hildy is one of *the* greatest character actresses working onstage and on-screen today. I'm sure you remember her from *The Butcher and the Angel*—it absolutely *swept* Cannes and Sundance. We are *very* lucky to be working with her."

*Is Ted already assuming I'll cast her?* Elizabeth wondered, her stomach sinking. The actress was probably in her late twenties or early thirties—a good five to ten years older than Ken. Under a black bowler hat flowed long, frizzy light brown hair that looked as if Hildy had fallen asleep on a crimping iron. She was wearing a brown tweed suit jacket and a wide black tie; the collar of her white dress shirt was turned up, and its cuffs hung loose out of the rolled-up sleeves of her jacket. Her untucked shirt and her brown tweed dress slacks both looked rumpled. *Is she really right for Phoebe?* Elizabeth wondered dubiously.

"Charmed, I'm *sure*," Hildy trilled, her voice carrying through the theater. She clasped her hands and hugged them to her chest. "I am so *thrilled* to work on your production, Elizabeth." She dragged the word *thrilled* into four syllables.

"Isn't this great?" Ted enthused as Elizabeth stood speechless. "We're going to have a real professional on board. And now that the casting's in place, we can get started rehearsing. Listen up, people!"

As Ted began calling out directions Elizabeth stood gaping at Hildy. *I can't say I don't want her— Ted would be furious,* she thought helplessly. *But she's not the type I pictured for the part at* all!

"Which chakra is this one for again?" Tom asked, holding up a vial of amber-colored essential oil.

Tish glanced over her shoulder from where she was mixing up a guava-oatmeal paste at the kitchen work island. "That's for the *vishuddha* chakra, which rules the throat—that would be Mr. Deming's sandalwood. If you're looking for Ms. Santangelo's jasmine-rosewood blend, it's in the bottle with the purple label over there."

"Oh, right, purple is for power . . . is that it?" Tom reached for the bottle and turned it over curiously in his hands.

"Yes, the *manipura* chakra," Tish explained. "You're really getting into aromatherapy, aren't you, dear?"

"Well, yeah, kind of," Tom confessed. "I never realized what a science it is. I'm not sure I believe everything, but it's pretty fascinating."

Tish wiped her hands on a dish towel and came to sit across from him at the kitchen table. "Scorpios have such wonderfully probing minds," she remarked thoughtfully. "They love prying into secrets, especially the mysteries of life . . . sources of power and energy. I'm sure you're a great journalist—uncovering abuses of power is your specialty, right?"

"Yes!" Tom exclaimed in surprise. "You could tell that?"

Tish nodded sagely. "Remind me to give *you* some of that *manipura* blend when I do your treatment." She sorted through a few of the bottles on the table before the doorbell rang. Tish jumped up and scurried out of the kitchen, returning a minute later with a tall, strikingly beautiful African American woman who had thick dreadlocks and a ring in her nose. "Halima Santangelo, this is Tom Watts—he's filling in for Zora," Tish explained. "Tom, could you get Ms. Santangelo her self-actualization blend, please?"

"It's nice to meet you, Tom," Halima said with a friendly smile. In her flowing purple-and-yellow daisy-patterned dress, she looked funky and spiritual at the same time. Like the eclectic handful of clients who had come in earlier, she was definitely *not* the flaky New Age type Tom had been expecting.

*This is like a whole community I never knew existed,* Tom reflected as he handed Halima the brown recycled paper bag that contained her individually tailored blend of herbs and essential oils. After all the rejections he'd experienced in his job search, it was nice to feel accepted and respected by Tish and her clients.

"Good luck with your chakras," Tom called as Halima left with her bag.

Tish gave him an approving look. "You've really

196

helped me out today," she told him. "I admit, I was a little worried at first that you might not have the right attitude toward the work, but you've really brought some good energy to the treatments."

"Thanks!" Tom beamed. "I'm actually having a lot of fun."

"Well, it shows." Tish reached across the table and gave Tom's hand a motherly squeeze. "You and I really work well together. We must have some good synastry in our astrological charts."

"Must be," Tom agreed, although he wasn't sure exactly what she was talking about. *She probably just means that we get along well,* he speculated. Tish seemed to have adopted a maternal attitude toward him; since Tom had lost his own parents, that kind of support meant everything. *I do feel connected to Tish,* he realized. *And to something bigger—almost . . . cosmic!*

"I don't want to see you get hurt, Phoebe. So I'm taking you off the story!" Ken Deal looked up expectantly from his script.

"You can't do that," Hildy Muldman breathed in a whisper-soft voice, touching her wrist to her forehead like the heroine of a Victorian novel. "I'm sticking with this case until—"

"OK, hang on," Elizabeth interjected from her seat in the front row. "Hildy, I'm sorry to break your flow again, but your voice isn't really projecting. Do you think you could take it up a notch and add a little bit of anger?"

Hildy closed her eyes and nodded painfully, as if

the effort would be too much. In the past hour of rehearsal Elizabeth had come to learn that Hildy preferred not to respond verbally to direction unless absolutely necessary. Talking prevented her from "finding her center."

"All right, then why don't we take it from 'You can't do that,' Hildy," Elizabeth suggested. "And . . . action!"

Hildy's eyes snapped open, and her face contorted into a mask of anguish. "You *can't* do *that!*" she cried, trilling the words in a theatrical vibrato that sounded almost as if she were about to burst into song. "I'm sticking with this case until we blow it wide open!" She punctuated the line with a loud sob.

"Hold it right there for a second," Elizabeth said wearily. "Hildy, I'm not sure you're really hitting the right note for this scene. At this point Phoebe's too far into her investigation to turn back. Not only that, but she's a strong, independent woman. So Gavin calling her off the story is like waving a red flag. She's *angry*—she's *yelling* at Gavin, not lamenting."

Hildy heaved an exasperated sigh. "Well, you *see*, Elizabeth, I just have this *feeling*. I just get this *vibe* that Phoebe is really quite fragile underneath all her bravado. She's really just a delicate hothouse flower, trying to blossom in a cold, masculine world. That's where I'm locating these feelings of pain and sadness."

Elizabeth glanced over at Ken and saw that his jaw was set in a grim, resigned line. *He must be as frustrated as I am,* Elizabeth realized, hoping Ken was a good enough actor to hide his attitude during his scenes with Hildy.

Although—or possibly *because*—she was such an acclaimed actress, Hildy Muldman seemed impelled to argue with every one of Elizabeth's directions. And when she wasn't arguing, she was affecting some of the most bizarre character traits Elizabeth had *never* seen in any person, real or fictional. *Fragile and delicate indeed!* Elizabeth thought hotly. She felt like shouting, *I may be just a student, but I wrote the darn play—I think I would know what the character is like!*

Elizabeth pasted an encouraging smile on her face. "I'm really glad you're feeling a connection with Phoebe," she said, choosing her words as carefully as she could. "But could you just try to go with me on this one? This is a pivotal scene—we need to be able to feel the way Gavin and Phoebe's passion for their work intersects with their passion for each other. If we don't have that"—Elizabeth's shoulders sagged—"there's essentially no point to the play. So do you think you could locate a little anger?" *I know where I can find some right about now!* she added silently.

"*Fine,*" Hildy huffed, as if Elizabeth had just ordered her to scrub out the Maxwell's stalls. "My instincts were good enough for Woody Allen, but I guess they're not good enough for you. I'll look for some anger, but I'm going to need a few minutes to regroup. All this quibbling has made me lose my center."

Elizabeth fought the impulse to tell Hildy where exactly she could go look for her center. "OK, let's take five," she said resignedly. "I'm sure we could *all* use a break."

Ken immediately stalked off the stage. Hildy remained in place, closed her eyes, and began massaging her temples as if she were channeling Sir Laurence Olivier.

*I'll go call Tom—he'll calm me down,* Elizabeth decided, heading for the lobby. *After I talk to someone who speaks my language, I'm sure I'll be able to laugh about this.*

When she reached the lobby, Elizabeth fished a quarter from her purse and dropped it into the pay phone. Tom answered on the first ring.

"Tish Ellenbogen's residence. Healing through aromatherapy and essential oils."

"Tom? Is that you?" It was definitely his voice, but Elizabeth couldn't quite make out his greeting. "Tom, I am *so* glad you're there. You have *no* idea what kind of day I'm having!"

"I'm having an amazing day too," Tom responded, sounding much more chipper than he had when Elizabeth had left him parked in front of the TV that morning. "I've been helping Tish out with her aromatherapy, and I'm really starting to get the hang of it! You wouldn't *believe* what I've learned today, Liz—it's really incredible stuff."

"That's great, Tom," Elizabeth answered, feeling a little let down. "Listen, I'm calling from a pay phone at the theater, so I can't stay on long. I just wanted to tell you that I love you and I miss you. I'm having kind of a rough day—"

"Gee, Liz, that's terrible," Tom said in a sympathetic voice. "The atmosphere must be really negative."

Gratified, Elizabeth felt her shoulders relax slightly. *Of course Tom understands,* she thought, relieved. *He's always there for me.*

"If you're having trouble communicating," Tom continued, "you could try stimulating the throat chakra, the *vi*—the *vishuddha*. It's a powerful chakra for writers since it can free you to express yourself when you're feeling blocked. If you want, I could mix up some herbs and essential oils for you and have everything ready when you get home." He paused. "It'd be really sensual, Liz," he added in a lower voice.

Elizabeth was momentarily speechless. "Tom . . . are you *possessed?*" she demanded finally. "What are you *talking* about?"

There was a loud exhalation of breath on the other end of the line. "Listen, Liz, I realize you've absorbed a lot of stressful vibrations, but we have a client coming in. We'll talk about your day later, OK?"

"Fine," Elizabeth snapped. "I had to go anyway."

*Has the whole world gone insane?* she wondered as she hung up the phone. *Or is it just me?*

"Take *that!* And *that!* And how 'bout some of *this?*" As Jessica thumped the punching bag with all her might she could feel her anger and aggression melting into pure energy.

"You want a piece of me?" she taunted the bag. "Yeah, you *wish!*" She jabbed out first with her right, then with her left, just the way Al had taught her. Jessica had been boxing for less than an hour, but already the stance was practically second nature. Her fists flew in time to the swinging of the bag as she hopped from foot to foot in an adrenaline-fueled dance.

"Wakefield, would you stop teasing that punching bag?" Annette called from a few yards away, where she was flirtatiously sparring with Al. "Why don't you pick on something that can stick up for itself?"

"No way," Jessica panted between punches. "I know what I'm doing. After all, *I'm* the *natural* here."

"Remember to keep your head low, Miss Natural," Al pointed out, "or you're going to get your block knocked off."

"For *now* I'll keep my head down," Jessica announced, feeling giddy with strength as she swaggered in front of the punching bag. "But I'll be holding it up high when I kick Pruitt's bony—"

Suddenly the door of the gym flew open with a loud crash. Jessica's words died on her lips as she realized that the uniformed figure silhouetted in the doorway belonged to Pruitt herself.

"So," Pruitt seethed, advancing by long strides across the wooden floor. Each thud of her heavy boots on the floorboards sounded like a death knell. "I was wondering where you pathetic grunts

202

ran off to. Couldn't handle the forty laps, huh?"

The room was silent. Jessica didn't dare breathe. She desperately wished that a hole would open in the earth and swallow her.

"Well, I'll take that as a yes," Pruitt snarled. Steam was practically rising from her cap. "You all make me *sick!*" she shrieked. "This is absolutely the *last* act of insubordination I will tolerate. Harris, Polanco, Vernon, Wakefield, you're all assigned overnight guard duty!"

*Did she say* overnight? *As in sleep deprivation?* Jessica bit back her cry of protest. There was only one thing she feared more than spending a cold, sleepless night alone with the swamp creatures, and that was making Pruitt even madder than she already was.

Pruitt turned her blazing eyes on the boxing instructor. "I'm *especially* disappointed in *you,* Al," Pruitt growled. "As a professional, you should have reported these disobedient recruits immediately. Rest assured that I will be bringing this matter to the attention of top brass. And if I have anything to say about it, you'll be dishonorably discharged!"

Al seemed to shrink back for a moment, then visibly drew himself up to his full height. He looked Pruitt in the eye, a glint of challenge in his dark eyes. "Go ahead," he said evenly. "I haven't done anything wrong."

Jessica sucked in her breath as Pruitt's whole body seemed to bristle. In the space of a second her face went from red to almost purple.

"You'll be *very* sorry you said that," Pruitt

hissed. "You'll *all* be sorry you messed with me—I'm going to make your pathetic lives even more miserable than they already are!"

As she spoke she lifted her fist menacingly in the air, then brought it down hard against Jessica's punching bag. The bag swung wildly out, and before Jessica could react, it barreled into her with full force. The next thing she knew, Jessica was sprawled out on the floor, pain shooting through her back. She gasped for breath, momentarily winded from the impact.

Dazed, Jessica raised herself up on her elbows in time to see Pruitt's figure disappear out the door. *I was so determined to show Pruitt that I'm tough enough to hack it*, she recalled despairingly as tears of pain and humiliation stung her eyes. *But I can't take much more of this abuse!*

"OK, that was my last appointment of the day," Tish announced cheerfully as the front door closed behind a middle-aged man with a long gray ponytail. "Let's start your stress-release treatment right away. I have tickets for an experimental performance art piece in Soho, and I've heard the artist is verbally abusive to latecomers."

"OK by me," Tom agreed. "Can I help you get set up?"

"No, no, you sit. You're a client now, not an assistant." Tish gestured toward the dining-room table, by the windows of her large front room. "Let's do it in here, all right? I find that the view of the park is very soothing to tired urban souls."

Tish hurried into the kitchen without waiting for a response, and Tom obediently took a seat at the table. A moment later she reappeared carrying a few vials and a small black velvet pouch. Tom watched, fascinated, as she set the vials on the dining-room table and produced from the velvet bag several small shiny-smooth pink stones.

"Rose quartz," Tish explained as she arranged the stones in a semicircle around Tom. "To stimulate the heart chakra and the release of soul-centered energy." She reached for a book of matches on the table and lit a cone of incense in a metal dish.

"Is that what you think is causing me stress?" Tom asked. "The heart chakra?"

Tish nodded solemnly as she took the seat opposite Tom. "I'm getting a strong sense that you're feeling blocked when it comes to matters of the heart. Something is keeping you from expressing your true feelings of love, and that tension is eating away at you."

*Something's blocking me from expressing my love, all right,* Tom thought wryly. *And her name is Elizabeth Wakefield!* He couldn't believe how accurate Tish's flaky New Age interpretations really were. Somehow she'd picked up on the fact that he and Elizabeth were going through a major turning point in their relationship. *Or at least I'm trying for one,* he added.

"Tom, let me ask you this—how are things with you and Elizabeth?" Tish asked as if she had read his mind. "Is that the source of the tension I'm reading in your aura?"

"Well," Tom admitted, "we love each other a lot, and we're totally committed, but there *have* been a few . . . miscommunications lately. We're kind of . . . deciding where to go with our relationship."

Tish nodded knowingly as she opened a vial of clear liquid. A lilac scent wafted across the table. "For what it's worth, you two seem very solid to me," she remarked. "I think it was wonderful of you to have so much respect for Elizabeth and her work that you would cross the country for her. But I know that deep relationships like yours often go through crises." She handed Tom the open vial across the table. "Here, dot this on your pulse points: behind your ears, your neck, your wrists."

Tom accepted the vial and pressed it against his wrist. *She's right—I did do a lot for Elizabeth,* he realized. *Why is it that Tish is more appreciative of that than Liz is?*

"I don't know if I would call it a crisis, exactly," he said slowly, rubbing his wrists together. "But we're not sure we have the same . . . needs."

Tish shook her head sympathetically as she unscrewed another vial, this one a dark, soy-sauce-like liquid with a woodsy scent. "To me you *seem* very sensitive to Elizabeth's needs," she observed, passing the vial to Tom. "Here, this is for your temples. Anyway, I'm sure that your relationship will get back on track. Maybe you both just need to give a little."

*I've done nothing* but *give!* Tom wanted to shout. But he decided that an outburst of anger wouldn't be conducive to stress release.

"I *try*," he said carefully as he massaged his temples. "But there are some things that Elizabeth just doesn't want to be flexible about. Or else she just doesn't trust me enough to take a chance."

Tish's forehead creased with concern. "Well, Geminis are always of two minds. But I would think that with the level of commitment you've shown, Elizabeth would feel safe trusting you. Especially since her heart chakra shines through so powerfully in her personality."

"You'd *think* that," Tom echoed bitterly. "But I guess she doesn't see it that way since *my* heart chakra is so messed up."

In spite of the oils that were tingling on his skin, Tom felt his tension and frustration mounting. Tish's words had really put things in perspective. He *had* given Elizabeth more than enough reason to trust him. He'd been flexible and giving above and beyond the call of duty. *I even uprooted my life—gave up a great job and an apartment of my own,* Tom recalled mournfully. *How many guys would do that for their girlfriends?*

"See, the keys to the heart chakra are unconditional love, trust, acceptance, and freedom from expectations," Tish explained, but Tom was barely listening.

*I'm not going to put up with this hot-and-cold stuff much longer,* he resolved. *It's humiliating!* He screwed the cap back on the vial and set it down on the table with slightly more force than was necessary. *It's about time Liz gave me a little credit!*

"Tom?" Tish was holding out a vial of amber liquid. "Are you ready for your sandalwood?"

"Uh, no, thanks." Tom shook his head, grimacing. "I appreciate you going to all this trouble, Tish, but I'm afraid the treatment isn't exactly working. To tell you the truth, I feel more stressed out than ever!"


"Ugh—*what* a day." Elizabeth groaned as she collapsed through the doorway of Tish's apartment. "I'm so glad you're home, Tom, because once I sit down, I don't think I'll be able to get back up."

"Well, then, you're in luck." Tom tossed aside his newspaper and patted the spot beside him on the couch. "In addition to being handsome, charming, and a great kisser, I happen to give a mean back rub."

Elizabeth smiled gratefully as she sank down onto the couch and eased her swollen feet out of her brown sling-back sandals. After a day of being made to feel like a naive, incompetent idiot, it was nice to be pampered by her doting boyfriend. "That sounds so wonderful, I'm not even going to argue about the 'handsome and charming' thing," she declared, turning her back to him.

Tom angled himself so that he was sitting directly behind Elizabeth. She felt him lift her ponytail off the nape of her neck. Then his lips were softly brushing the bare skin by her spaghetti strap. Elizabeth felt a delicious thrill run through her

208

body as her exhausting day receded further and further in her mind.

"I notice you're not taking objection to the 'good kisser' part," Tom said huskily, his breath warm on her neck.

"Never," Elizabeth murmured, tilting her head back and twisting slightly so that Tom's searching lips found hers. She closed her eyes and felt the last of her tension slipping away as she melted into a slow, deep kiss that seemed to last forever. *Tom always knows how to make me feel better,* she thought dreamily. *Thank goodness he seems to have gotten over his attack of New Age–itis!*

When they broke apart, Tom's hands began kneading her shoulders. Elizabeth let her head slump as the pressure of his fingers loosened the knots in her muscles. "That feels so good," she moaned. "I don't ever want to go back to the Maxwell—I just want to stay here with you."

"So tell me about your day," Tom urged. "What happened at the theater that made you so upset?"

"Well, *first* of all, the producer basically *forced* me to cast this actress who is *so* wrong for the part," Elizabeth began angrily, her muscles tensing at the memory. "And she wouldn't stop bickering with me *all day* over her weird interpretations of the play. But the worst thing was, I barely knew how to argue with her since my play is a total *mess!*"

"Liz, don't say that. Your play is great!" Tom insisted.

Elizabeth shook her head. "I don't know anymore. Ted had a million criticisms, and I made lots of changes in the script, but they just don't seem to fit with everything else! I don't know whether to scrap the whole thing and start from scratch or try to convince Ted that my play was fine the way it was."

She heaved an exasperated sigh, her mind a jumble of questions about dialogue, blocking, and character development. *What if I break my back rewriting the whole play and then it ends up being as pretentious and ridiculous as Claire's?* Elizabeth worried.

"Liz," Tom said in a low voice, "I know a way to take your mind off your play." His hands slipped from her shoulders, and he wrapped his arms around her, pressing her back against his chest.

"What?" Elizabeth asked distractedly. *I just want to put on my play the way I wrote it!* she continued thinking. *If it was good enough for the Foundation, why isn't it good enough for Ted?*

Tom rested his chin in the crook of her neck. "Tish went downtown to see an art installation, and she said she would probably grab a late supper with friends afterward," he said meaningfully. "So it looks like we have the place to ourselves tonight. I was thinking maybe we could, uh, adjourn to the bedroom."

Elizabeth snapped out of her reverie. "Tom, *please,*" she snapped, struggling free of his embrace. "Is that *all* you ever think about? Do you even care about anything I'm saying? Or were you just asking me about my day to charm me into bed?" She turned around and saw Tom's face darken. As soon as the words were out of her mouth she regretted them—but it was too late.

"I can't *believe* you, Liz," Tom cried, outraged. "What the hell do I have to *do* to convince you that I'm not just *using* you? I mean, it should be obvious by now how much I care about you! How much longer do I have to *wait?*"

Elizabeth's lower lip quivered. There was an edge in Tom's voice that she had never heard before. "Tom, I—I'm just not sure this is the right time, OK? I have a lot on my mind, and—"

"Well, when *is* it going to be the right time, Liz?" Tom jumped up from the couch and stood hovering over her, his eyes blazing. "When are you going to think about what *I* want for once? I have needs too, you know!"

"Tom, I *do* care about what you want!" Elizabeth cried, her eyes filling with tears. "It's just that th-this is a big decision for me, Tom! Please try to understand—"

"I've done nothing *but* understand!" Tom thundered, jabbing an accusing finger in her direction. "It was a big decision for *me* to come all the way here for *you,* and it's like you don't even care! I sacrificed *everything* I had back in California for you—*everything!* And all I've gotten back is one humiliating rejection after another!"

"Tom, that's not fair," Elizabeth sobbed. "I'm not *rejecting* you, I—"

"Oh, really, Liz? It sure *seems* that way. And I'm sick and tired of it." Tom gave her one long, cold look. Then he turned and stormed toward the door.

"Where are you going?" Elizabeth cried weakly. She felt as if she'd just had the wind knocked out of her, and there was no hope of ever getting it back.

*"Out,"* Tom growled, slamming the door behind him.

Elizabeth sat frozen on the couch for a minute before running to her room and throwing herself facedown on the bed. "How could he *do* that to me?" she moaned. "After everything he said about not pressuring me!" Her heart felt as if it had been shattered into a million pieces.

*At least now I know I was right to wait,* Elizabeth thought bitterly as she sobbed into her pillow. *My relationship with Tom isn't as solid as I thought it was—not at all!*

# Chapter
# Fifteen

"I'll have a shot of tequila," Tom told the bartender in his most macho voice. He swiveled on his bar stool and surveyed the seedy pool hall where he'd ended up after walking the Upper West Side for what seemed like hours. It was a dark, smoky room that smelled of stale beer and cigarettes and contained only a bar, an ancient jukebox blaring classic rock, and a few scrappy pool tables.

*Just the kind of place Elizabeth would hate,* Tom reflected with a malicious, empty satisfaction as he tossed a couple of bills on the bar. As a matter of fact, he didn't see a single woman anywhere—the bar and pool tables were packed with clusters of rowdy guys. *Fine with me—I could use a little male bonding. After the grief Elizabeth has brought me, I don't even want to* think *about the opposite sex.*

He picked up his shot glass from the greasy

wooden bar and drained it in one fiery swig that burned a noxious trail down his throat. Tom shuddered violently and fought the impulse to gag. A heavyset, dark-haired guy about his age was sitting a few stools away, regarding him with an amused smirk.

"Women problems?" the guy asked Tom with a tip of his baseball cap.

"Yeah, how'd you know?" Tom asked, startled by the man's perception as well as queasy from the tequila.

"Well, you don't look like much of a drinker," the guy explained, grinning. "And there's only one thing that can make a man pathetic enough to choke down a tequila shot: a woman."

Tom grimaced. "Good call. I just had a huge fight with my girlfriend."

"The name's Rocco." The guy extended his hand to Tom.

"Tom Watts." As Tom shook Rocco's hand four burly jock types came up behind him. Two clapped him on the shoulder, and one twisted the baseball cap on his head.

"Hey, Rocc-o-o-o," one of the guys yelled. "Hurry up with those beers! Are we gonna play some more pool or what?"

"You bet! Hey, you guys, this is Tom." Rocco stood up and looked at Tom. "Tom, you wanna hang with us, have a few rounds?"

Tom hesitated momentarily. He'd come in planning to have a quick drink and take a few minutes to get his head together. *But it's not like I have a* reason *to get home early,* he realized. *I don't have a job to wake up for, and I certainly don't have a girl-friend to get home to!*

Tom smiled broadly. "Sure—the night is young," he declared. "I'm up for anything!"


Jessica felt as if lead weights were attached to her feet. Every step she took required tremen-dous effort, yet it seemed as if she were hardly moving forward at all. Even late at night the FSSA compound was covered by a humid blanket; trudging across it felt like wading through neck-deep water.

*I don't even have a gun,* she thought foggily, waving her nightstick in front of her face in a vain effort to create a breeze. *It's not like I'm really "guarding" anything—if someone* did *break into the compound, I'd be dead meat!*

As Jessica patrolled the rows of barracks she saw a flicker of movement in the darkness a couple of feet ahead of her. Her heart in her throat, Jessica gripped her nightstick tightly in both hands and slowly raised it over her head.

"Chill, Wakefield! It's just me!" Bev's voice rang out.

"Phew! Am I glad," Jessica breathed as she fell into step beside Bev. "I was scared stiff for a minute there."

"You and me both," Bev agreed. "This overnight guard thing is so bogus."

"Pruitt's trying to get us to give in," Jessica said darkly. "And I hate to admit it, but I'm starting to

215

think it's working. I mean, we've only been here a couple of days and she's practically run me into the ground. How am I going to make it through a whole summer?"

Bev shook her head. "I don't know. I don't know how *any* of us are going to manage. All my savings are going toward tuition—if Pruitt gets us kicked out or makes us quit, there's nowhere else for me to go."

"Why does Pruitt go out of her way to ruin our lives?" Jessica asked in frustration.

Bev shrugged helplessly. "Pretty much the only word that comes to mind is *evil*. Listen, what do you say we go look for Sunshine and Annette? I have a feeling there's safety in numbers."

"Sounds like a plan."

They found Sunshine and Annette sitting huddled together on the ground outside the mess hall. Annette was asleep with her head resting on Sunshine's shoulder, but she opened her eyes as Jessica and Bev approached.

"Hey, guys," Sunshine said softly. "Did you want to be first in line for coffee tomorrow too?"

"No, we were looking for you," Bev said with an amused grin. "We wanted to make sure all four of us were together in case Pruitt pulled any other stunts."

"What could she possibly pull besides making us grovel in the dirt all night?" Annette grumbled, her voice thick with sleep.

"I'm sure she could think of *something*," Jessica asserted. "I don't know why she hates me so much, but obviously she'll stop at nothing to make *all* of us miserable."

"I wish we could report her or something." Annette sighed. "But she has so much clout here. There's no way we could prove she's punished us unfairly."

"Nobody would stand up for us—everyone's terrified of her," Sunshine added with a puff of cigar smoke.

"I want to take her *down!*" Bev slammed her fists together. "There's got to be *some* way we can nail her scrawny butt."

"But what?" Jessica asked gloomily. "She has all the power here. If we try to get revenge, she'll just punish us again." She sank down to the ground beside Annette and Sunshine. "Face it, Pruitt has us in the palm of her hand. She's watching us squirm and loving it— and there's *nothing* we can do."

"Chug! Chug! Chug!" Rocco and his pals chanted. They pumped their fists in the air as Bud, an enormous muscle-bound guy with a crew cut, downed an entire mug of beer in one guzzle. When Bud had drained every drop, the crowd around him erupted into whoops.

Tom, bent over the pool table, made his shot and straightened up, shaking his head. *What a bunch of fascinating conversationalists,* he thought sarcastically. It was almost 2 A.M.; as Tom had recently learned, nightlife in New York didn't start to pick up until around midnight. As the night wore on and the pool hall grew more crowded, Tom's new drinking buddies had grown more and more rowdy and boorish. Whenever a young woman walked by, they fell all over each other in a noisy catcalling contest and then bought another round at the bar to congratulate themselves on their studly "conquest."

Tom had quit drinking after a couple of beers, realizing how pathetic it was for him to try drowning his sorrows in alcohol. At this point he was stone-cold sober, totally depressed about the state of his relationship with Elizabeth, and feeling something halfway between boredom and disgust at the company of his new "friends." *What a sad excuse for male bonding,* he thought morosely. *I feel more like an anthropologist living among the apes!*

"Aaay, Tommy!"

When Tom felt a clammy hand drop on his shoulder, he turned to see Rocco with his arm around a buxom blonde who was about to burst out of her red vinyl minidress.

"Tommy, this is Fawn," Rocco explained, grinning from ear to ear. "Ain't she something?" He leaned into her as if she were the only thing preventing him from falling over.

"She's *something,* all right," Tom echoed, mesmerized by how Fawn's fire-engine-red lipstick was bordered by a chalky silver line.

As he stared at the cheap-looking woman Tom wondered what had possessed him to risk losing Elizabeth. The memory of his words and actions made him feel like he was as much of a sexist jerk as the leering idiots around him.

Fawn tittered. "Rocky, honey, I'm going to powder my nose." She wriggled out from under his arm. "I'll meetcha at the bar."

"You hurry back!" Rocco called, waving his arm and swaying unsteadily. Tom felt Rocco shift his balance to the hand that was still clamped on his shoulder. Tom staggered under the weight and found his bearings.

Rocco leaned his face close to Tom's. "Does she have a nice rack on her or *what?*" he loudly whispered, his breath toxic. "Whaddya bet I get a coupla drinks in her and she gives me a little sugar, huh? Huh?"

Tom's gut wrenched, and he had the urge to punch Rocco right in his leering, booze-reddened face. But it seemed somehow unfair to knock out a man who was having enough trouble standing as it was. Instead Tom silently steered Rocco toward the bar and pushed him onto an empty stool.

*I hate hearing men talk about women like they're pieces of meat,* Tom thought as he threw a few bills onto the bar to cover his tab. *Especially tonight, after the way I acted with Liz.* The fact that he had actually heard a little of himself in Rocco's lecherous slur made Tom feel sick with shame.

True, he hadn't resorted to truly contemptible ploys like plying Elizabeth with alcohol. *But I did put pressure on her,* Tom admitted as he headed toward the door. *How could I accuse* Elizabeth *of not wanting a mature relationship when* I'm *the immature one? Real men don't pressure women into doing things they're not ready for! No matter what I've done, she doesn't "owe" me anything.*

Tom felt panic rise in his throat as he fought his way through the crowded, smoky pool hall. *Even if I beg her forgiveness, will she ever trust me again?* he wondered apprehensively. *What if she can't forget how I turned on her?*

He burst through the door of the pool hall onto the street and took a deep breath. Spotting an approaching yellow cab, Tom raised his hand to flag it. But as the taxi slowed, Tom flashed back to his last couple of New York cab rides. Already he'd made a sizable dent in his savings, blown his chance for a romantic evening with Elizabeth, and sustained a minor injury. After everything that had happened tonight, he really wasn't in the mood for any more hair-raising experiences.

*I'd better walk home,* Tom resolved, waving the cabbie on. *I don't want to die without telling Liz I'm sorry!*

"Tom, I don't think we should see each other anymore," Elizabeth said in a choked whisper. "I love you, but I'm just not ready for the kind of relationship you want."

The words hung in the silence of the darkened bedroom. Elizabeth let out a low whimper and rolled onto her side, convulsing with sobs. She couldn't imagine what it would be like to actually *tell* Tom it was over—even when she practiced, it just sounded wrong.

*I don't want to break up with Tom,* Elizabeth admitted forlornly. *But I don't see what other choice I have if he won't stop pressuring me.*

Elizabeth flopped miserably onto her back and fingered the gold bangle around her wrist as if to convince herself that the loving boyfriend who'd given it to her still existed. She'd been lying in bed, crying her eyes out, for hours. Despite her exhaustion Elizabeth couldn't seem to fall sleep. Every time she closed her eyes, she pictured Tom's anger-hardened face staring daggers at her, bringing with it a fresh round of tears.

A soft knock at the door made Elizabeth hope she hadn't woken Tish with her sobbing. "Who is it?" she called quietly.

"It's me, Tom," came a low, muffled voice. "Can I come in?"

Elizabeth stiffened and pulled the covers protectively around her. She hadn't even heard Tom come in. If it was as late as she thought, he'd probably been out for hours, carousing or brawling or who knew what. *What if he wants to pick up where we left off?* Elizabeth thought, a sinking feeling in the pit of her stomach.

"Whatever you have to say to me, you can say through the door," she declared. "I don't want to be alone with you right now."

There was silence for a moment; then Elizabeth heard Tom sigh. "OK, I deserve that," he conceded, the defeat in his voice apparent even through the door. "But please hear me out, Liz. I swear I won't lay a finger on you—just let me say this face-to-face, and I'll leave you alone."

221

Elizabeth exhaled deeply. "Come in; it's open," she admitted grudgingly.

As the door opened, Elizabeth rolled onto her side so her back would face Tom. The mattress springs creaked as he sat down on the edge of her bed. She could feel his weight on the mattress and the tension of his presence in the room, but she couldn't bring herself to look at him.

Tom cleared his throat. "Liz, first of all, you have every right to be mad. I mean, not that you need me to tell you that . . . but I want you to know that *I* know how wrong I was. I'm ashamed of myself."

Elizabeth gradually released her tight grip on the blanket, and she dabbed at her tears with the corners of the sheets. Not trusting herself to speak, she waited for Tom to continue.

"Liz, I love you more than I can say," Tom went on. "I just wanted to be close to you, and I crossed some lines that I shouldn't have even gone near. I didn't respect your wishes or your needs, and that was really wrong. I'm sorry—so sorry."

Elizabeth felt her heart begin to melt.

"Nothing can excuse how I acted, but . . ." She felt Tom's hand on her shoulder. "Liz, for crying out loud, would you just look at me?"

Relenting, Elizabeth rolled over and met Tom's eyes. In the moonlight she could see that he looked haggard and haunted. His brow furrowed in concern as he scanned her tear-streaked face.

"Go on," she urged in a strangled voice.

"Please don't cry, Liz." Tom tenderly rubbed

her shoulder. "I just wanted you to know that I'm truly, deeply sorry, and it will never happen again. It kills me to realize how upset I've made you. From now on I promise not to abuse our trust— we won't even mention sex again unless *you* bring it up."

"Oh, Tom . . ." Elizabeth smiled through her tears, reached for Tom's wrist, and pulled him down onto the bed beside her. "I love you so much. Of course I accept your apology."

"I love *you*, Liz." Tom put his arm around her. "I never meant to hurt you. I promise I'll make it up to you—we still have the whole summer ahead of us."

"I believe you." Elizabeth slipped her arm around Tom's waist and rested her head contentedly against his T-shirted chest. The rise and fall of his warm, broad chest against her cheek was rhythmic and soothing. "Such a nice boyfriend," she murmured sleepily.

"You're so sweet." Tom chuckled, stroking her hair. Elizabeth felt his hand slow down before coming to rest on the nape of her neck. The sound of his breath becoming deep and even was the last thing Elizabeth was aware of before she drifted off to a peaceful, dreamless sleep in Tom's arms.

# Chapter Sixteen

*I'm sure that my skills could prove useful to your team,* Tom typed on the keypad of his laptop computer. *I look forward to hearing from you at your earliest convenience. Best regards, Tom Watts.*

He saved his document and ran his fingers through his tangled hair, tensely surveying the screen. He'd woken up alone on Elizabeth's bed, fully clothed and on top of the covers, and panicked when he realized that it was a little before noon. Since he'd already lost valuable job-hunting time, Tom had gone directly into his room with the want ads and started cranking out cover letters.

Tom reached around to his back and scratched an itch underneath his T-shirt. *I'm in dire need of a shower,* he realized. He was overjoyed that things had worked out with Elizabeth, and sleeping with her—just literally *sleeping* with her—had been a nice way to solidify how close they were. But spending the night in jeans and shoes hadn't exactly done wonders for his sense of physical well-being. In fact, Tom felt as if every inch of his skin was crawling.

"I have to take a shower *now*," Tom said aloud, pushing his chair back from the large mahogany desk. It was impossible to concentrate on his resumes when he felt so grungy.

He walked down the hall to the bathroom and started the shower running. *As soon as I find a job, I'm taking Elizabeth out for a big, fancy dinner at some trendy restaurant,* Tom resolved as he shrugged his shirt over his head. *After all we've been through, I want the two of us to make a fresh start. No complications, no pressure—just the two of us enjoying our time together.*

As Tom undid the buckle of his pants he caught sight of his reflection in the rapidly fogging bathroom mirror—and froze.

"*No!*" Tom screamed. Every inch of his skin was bright pink—and covered in flaming red, raised blotches.


"Elizabeth! I'm so glad you're here!" Ted clasped his hands as if he really was thrilled to see her arrive at the theater for rehearsal. "Hildy and I were just discussing some *fabulous* ideas for the first scene."

Hildy nodded in earnest agreement. "We had a *marvelous* brainstorm about Phoebe—that it would *perfectly* capture her essence for her to literally dance around Gavin in the first scene." She swung her arms out in a kind of arabesque.

"A *dance?*" Elizabeth cried, caught off guard. She had come to the theater determined to hold her ground and had no idea how to respond to such an absurd suggestion.

"A delightful little ballet," Hildy clarified, raising her arms over her head in an arc and doing a little pirouette. In her brown tweed jacket and floor-length lavender floral-print jumpsuit, she looked in no way like a ballerina. "To show what a truly delicate blossom she is underneath it all."

Elizabeth's mouth dropped. For a moment she was speechless.

"Well, Elizabeth?" Ted prompted her. "Are you considering the dramatic potential of our idea?"

*I can't let this go on any longer,* Elizabeth resolved wearily. *So far I've had a miserable summer because I haven't stood up for myself. Well, from now on I'm making decisions and sticking to them—no matter what* anyone *says!*

Elizabeth lifted her chin and threw back her shoulders. "Ted, Hildy, I have something to say. I'm sure your idea has *lots* of . . . uh . . . dramatic potential. But the truth is, I'm not making any changes from my original draft. I appreciate all your notes, Ted, but they just don't fit the spirit of the play, and that is something I'm *not* willing to compromise." She took a deep breath. "My play earned me the fellowship the way *I* wrote it," she concluded, "and that's the way I'm going to put it on."

She waited for an indignant outburst, but none came. Hildy just rolled her eyes. And to Elizabeth's surprise, Ted nodded approvingly.

"Congratulations, Elizabeth," he announced in a thundering voice. "That's exactly what I *wanted* to hear. You must learn to trust your own judgment, to stand behind your own artistic choices. That is your *only* chance if you want to make it in the theater."

With that, Ted clapped briskly. "OK, people," he boomed. "Let's get moving—we have a lot to cover today. Claire, we'll be blocking your play first. Places, everybody!"

Elizabeth stood recovering her bearings as the room came to life around her. She was relieved that Ted supported her decision but vaguely disappointed that the revelation she'd agonized over had been such a nonevent. Nobody seemed to be looking at her with new respect; in fact, nobody was even looking at her.

*I guess I should be proud—that* was *a breakthrough,* Elizabeth reflected warily. *But Ted sure has a way of making it seem insignificant!*

"Remind me not to drink that stuff they call coffee ever again." Sunshine groaned, clutching her stomach as she pushed through the front door of the mess hall. "I'm practically bouncing off the walls as it is—I'd hate to see what would happen if I'd gotten more than twenty minutes of sleep."

"I'm all wound up too," Jessica agreed, following closely behind Sunshine. "You know, I think I stopped feeling tired around dawn—now I'm pretty much running on autopilot."

"Pruitt's treating us like prisoners of war," Bev

grumbled as they strolled across the compound. "I don't know if it's the coffee or the sleep deprivation, but I feel like I'm gonna snap if I don't blow off some steam."

"Let's stop by the gym and get a little more boxing practice," Jessica suggested. "We could work out some of our frustrations and tire ourselves out enough to nap for a while."

Annette coughed into her hand. "Sounds good to me," she said, batting her eyelashes innocently.

The others hooted with teasing laughter. "Girl, you are crushing *hard*," Bev declared. "Not that I blame you—Al is *tasty*. But at least spare us the pitiful attempts to be subtle."

Yet when they let themselves into the gym, Al was nowhere to be found. "Where do you think he is?" Annette asked anxiously as they laced up their gloves. "Do you guys think Pruitt had him suspended?"

"I doubt she could have done it that fast, but I wouldn't put it past her," Jessica replied, jabbing at a punching bag. "She must get some kind of sick thrill from ruining other people's lives. Look at the way she's running us ragged, trying to force us to drop out."

"It's not going to work!" Bev exclaimed hotly, punching her own bag with obvious force. "No matter how hard she tries, she can't keep me from graduating."

"Well, so far we haven't lost any points on our exercises," Sunshine observed. "But I can't exactly keep up peak performance much longer with Pruitt torturing us like this."

In Jessica's fatigued state the blur of the swinging punching bag was almost hypnotic. Blood singing in her ears, she fought to keep her eyes open, to keep boxing through her exhaustion. "Somebody needs to wipe up the pavement with that old witch," she yelled, picturing Pruitt's face on the punching bag to keep up her energy. "I'd like to show her . . . who's . . ."

Suddenly Jessica realized that the other three women had gone silent. She stopped jabbing and looked around. When the room stopped swaying, she saw that her friends were staring in dismay at something behind her.

Her heart sinking, Jessica slowly turned around to see Sergeant Pruitt standing in the middle of the gym, her hands clenched in fists at her sides, her face an ashen mask of white-hot fury. "So, *princess*," she seethed, her voice dripping venom. "You think you can take *me* on?"

Jessica's knees were weak, but she drew herself up to her full height and looked Pruitt right in the eye. "As a matter of fact, I *do*," Jessica asserted. "I'm a lot tougher than you think I am!"

Behind her one of her friends gasped.

"Oh, *really?*" Pruitt sneered. "I'd like to see you prove it! If you're such a hotshot, you should have no trouble beating *me* in a boxing match. We'll see who wipes up the floor with whom!"

"No trouble at all," Jessica confirmed, her heart in her throat. She had no idea what she was doing, but short of throwing herself at Pruitt's feet and begging for mercy, there was no turning back now.

"Fine." Pruitt's eyes gleamed with cold triumph. "You're going to regret you ever took me up on that challenge, princess." A malicious laugh escaped her thin lips. "You better hope there's enough makeup in that bag of yours to cover up a broken nose!"

With that, Pruitt spun on her heel and stormed out of the gym, slamming the door behind her so hard that the whole room vibrated. For a moment all four women stood in stunned silence. Then Bev screeched, "Wakefield, are you out of your *mind*?"

"I kind of got in over my head, huh?" Jessica admitted with a nervous little laugh. "I guess I wasn't really thinking straight. Well, I'll have a few days to practice, and—"

"You don't *understand*." Sunshine shook her head with a look of disbelief. "Pruitt's not just talking trash about broken noses. Didn't you know she was a Golden Gloves titleholder?"

"Golden . . . Gloves?" Jessica croaked. "Uh-oh!"

"Vince, your character represents the left wing, so you'll enter from stage left," Claire explained, "but the rest of you should sort of . . . *swoosh* in from the right." She leaned over to one side, stretching out her arms to illustrate what she meant. In her long-sleeved, flowing black dress she looked like a witch casting some kind of evil spell over the stage.

Elizabeth turned slightly in her third-row seat so none of the actors onstage could see her roll her eyes. She couldn't help being amused by Claire's bizarre idea of "blocking"—so far the only stage direction she'd given her cast was to file onstage and form a line. But Claire was acting more animated than Elizabeth had ever seen her; it was obvious that she was thrilled with her own work. Watching Claire's white-powdered, black-lined features transform into a look of giddy excitement was turning out to be the best entertainment Elizabeth had seen in New York so far.

Claire clapped. "OK, people, we're ready to *shock* the world of theater!" she exclaimed. "Places, everyone. Vince, you know your cue? You enter on *nothingness.*"

Vince Klee nodded somberly and turned to head offstage along with the other actors. *He almost looks . . . nervous,* Elizabeth observed, bewildered, as Claire paced manically in front of the stage. *But he's a major movie star! Why would he be nervous about a rehearsal for a student performance?*

After a minute Claire stopped pacing and clapped. "And . . . action!" she shouted.

Intrigued in spite of herself, Elizabeth leaned slightly forward in her seat.

"Thus we descend," Vince intoned loudly from offstage, "into the bowels of our very being. Into raw, primal *nothingness!*"

A moment later he poked his head out onstage. Vince hesitated, then slowly walked toward center stage, as did the rest of the cast.

Elizabeth stared, openmouthed, as the dozen or so actors and actresses formed a line onstage. "No!" she whispered, unable to believe her eyes. "No! She *couldn't* have!"

As the players shifted awkwardly in line Claire threw her head back and let out a yelp of triumph that echoed throughout the theater.

Elizabeth sat frozen with shock. Never in a million years had she expected to be confronted by the sight that now greeted her onstage. Every actor and actress in Claire's cast—including Vince Klee—was *stark naked!*

*Can Tom recover from his mystery illness—and find a job—before Elizabeth begins seeing even more of Vince Klee? Or is that less likely than Jessica's chances of escaping Pruitt's left hook? Find out in Sweet Valley University #40, PRIVATE JESSICA.*

You'll always remember your first love.